USA TODAY BESTSELLING AUTHOR
DALE MAYER

Handcuffs in the Heather

Lovely Lethal Gardens 8

HANDCUFFS IN THE HEATHER: LOVELY LETHAL GAR-
DENS, BOOK 8
Beverly Dale Mayer
Valley Publishing Ltd.

ISBN-13: 978-1-773362-05-2
Print Edition

Books in This Series:

About This Book

A new cozy mystery series from *USA Today* best-selling author Dale Mayer. Follow gardener and amateur sleuth Doreen Montgomery—and her amusing and mostly lovable cat, dog, and parrot—as they catch murderers and solve crimes in lovely Kelowna, British Columbia.

Riches to rags. ... Everything is under control, ... until it isn't. And Doreen's in the middle of it!

The four boxes of files Doreen inherited from journalist Bridgeman Solomon have already helped her solve one crime, and Doreen hopes they'll continue to assist her as she sticks her nose into future cases. But, when she stumbles over a pair of pink satin handcuffs in her standoffish neighbor Richard de Genaro's heather patch, it's hard to believe that those reporter's files could have anything useful to offer regarding that.

Doreen takes a look though, and soon she's headed down a merry trail of prostitution, embezzlement, and, of course, murder. But the minute the files suggest a connection to Doreen's specialty, a cold case, her beau and partner in crime, Corporal Mack Moreau, starts breathing down her neck.

With her trusty animals leading the way, Doreen sets out to find the connection between the reputable banker who died in an unsolved hit-and-run and the prostitute who owned the pink satin handcuffs. As Doreen puts it all together, even she is surprised at the outcome of her latest investigation.

Chapter 1

Friday Late Afternoon ...

"ALL YOU NEED to do now," Mack said, "is stay out of trouble."

Doreen shrugged. "How much trouble can I get in? I've been gardening all day, and I'm coming up to the big hydrangea bush. I can get in no trouble with that."

He just looked at her. "Hydrangeas?"

She shrugged. "Those big flowering plants. I promise I'll spend tomorrow working in my garden."

He stared at her in doubt, also noting how all three of her animals sat nearby, watching the exchange like a tennis match. They didn't seem disturbed at the discussion. They knew this was the usual exchange between Mack and Doreen.

She chuckled. "Of course I can't guarantee what I might find."

"You don't get to find anything," he said, a warning in his tone.

"Well, why not? There was a gun in the gardenias. Maybe I'll find ..." She stopped, pondered for a moment. "How about I find handcuffs in the hydrangeas?" she announced triumphantly.

"How about you don't? How about you just stop trying to find anything?" And, with that, he turned and stormed out.

Mutinously, she watched him walk out the front door, her traitorous animals trotting behind him, all wanting goodbye hugs or pats. She trailed behind him, her gaze falling on the wheelbarrow with the little bit of dirt left that she had "borrowed." She still had to return the last of it to her neighbor.

She picked up the handles to the wheelbarrow and pushed it to his house, her animal trio in tow. There she rapped on the door. When he opened it, glaring at her suspiciously, she said, "I just brought this back. I promise to get you some more to replace what I used."

He shook his head. "Don't bother. That's all extra anyway. It was outside because I'm supposed to spread it in the front garden but haven't gotten around to it." He glared at her animals.

Mugs, Thaddeus, and Goliath knew better than to ask Richard for a hug or a pat to the head and stayed close to Doreen.

"Put it right there." Richard pointed to a spot at the corner of the garage.

She nodded and said, "Well, thank you for the dirt I used." She lifted the wheelbarrow handles and dumped the last bit in a pile as he'd requested. As she turned the wheelbarrow around, she looked at the hydrangeas in his garden and said, "This garden is doing really well. And that heather is gorgeous. The hydrangea is looking lovely too."

"The hydrangea is nice. It's the blue-flowering variety."

As she studied the bush, she wondered out loud, "I'm

surprised that bush is so small though."

He shrugged. "It's been small since forever. I don't know why. Probably no room to grow against the house."

She wondered. "May I take a look?"

He stared at her suspiciously. "What could you possibly look at?"

But she eyed something flashing in the sunlight. Only it wasn't in the hydrangeas but rather in the blooming heather in front of the bigger bush. "Who knows? Something could be restricting the bush's root system." At least that gave her an excuse to get in the garden bed.

She crouched at the edge of the hydrangeas to where the heather had tangled up in something metallic.

Almost immediately she identified the item. She gasped, and then she laughed. Very carefully she scooped away the leaves and the mulch that had piled up over the years. Mugs, Thaddeus, and Goliath all stepped in to *help*. "Hey, guys, I've got this."

And, sure enough, she found a set of handcuffs, one of which was caught around the plant.

She sat back and howled with laughter. It wasn't handcuffs in the hydrangeas. Instead, it was handcuffs in the heather ...

Who'd have guessed this?

Even better that they were torn and very much worse-for-wear pink satin handcuffs ... She snickered.

Wait until she told Mack ...

Chapter 2

Friday Late Afternoon ...

DOREEN REACHED OVER with a nearby stick and carefully disentangled the metal object. It was caught up in the heather from deep underneath, half buried and half twisted in the greenery. Luckily both the cuffs were open and not clicked shut. Eventually she broke them free and held them up for her neighbor to see. She snickered again and, trying for a straight face, asked, "Did you lose these?"

Richard inspected the handcuffs, partially covered with what appeared to have once been a soft pink satin; only now they were soiled with dirt and stained over time. Embarrassed, he stared at her, his jaw dropping. "Those aren't mine," he squeaked, his face flushing bright red.

"Well, maybe not," Doreen said. "They're pink. Maybe your wife's?"

He was so irate it looked like he would stomp his foot. Instead he spun on his heel and roared, "Get that nastiness out of my yard!" Then, when he reached his doorway, he looked back and said, "You probably planted them there."

She stared at him in surprise. "Well, they're not mine. And it's obvious they've been here for a long time, long before I moved here. Who knew you were into kink behind closed doors?"

He slammed his door in her face.

She burst out laughing before mustering enough seriousness to leave. Calling her critters, she pushed the wheelbarrow with one hand and held the handcuffs with the other, still looped over the stick she'd poked them with. When she reached her house, she parked the wheelbarrow in her garage and took the handcuffs inside. She carefully laid them on a piece of paper towel and studied them. "Handcuffs in the heather," she said to herself. "Mack will never believe that."

Not that she was ready to tell him. It definitely wasn't a police issue but a sex-story issue. And, of course, that raised all kinds of interesting questions. She'd never really been exposed to sex toys, so this offered a whole new level of research. And she also expected all kinds of issues when doing that research with her own laptop. She had decent virus checkers, but she was bound to end up on porn sites. Not exactly what she considered her daily reading. Although, if that was all she had for issues, then whatever.

But relieved that her unpaid workday designated to helping the local police was more or less over, with the potential of a fire tamped down here at her house and with Steve caught and hopefully at the police station, Doreen opted for a hot cup of tea at the creek. It amazed her how the soothing sound of the water perked up her spirits and gave her energy instead of draining her. Right now, she didn't really want too much energy because she was looking forward to an early bedtime tonight. And considering what she'd been through these last few days, a hot bath and an early night would be perfect.

But she couldn't stop thinking about the handcuffs. What an odd place for them. Her neighbor had to be in his seventies. He had told Doreen that he had a wife, Sicily, yet Doreen had never seen Sicily. Doreen had heard that odd androgynous voice out in their backyard behind the tall wooden privacy fence every once in a while. So Doreen was never sure if she was speaking to Richard or to Sicily.

And Doreen wasn't even sure that *he* was a *he* or that Sicily was a *she*. Even if a *he*, maybe Richard was homosexual. She didn't have any problem with that. But, if the neighbor's partner was hiding away, that would explain why nobody ever saw them. In which case, maybe the handcuffs were theirs.

She smirked at the idea. Something was very delightful about the thought of her grumpy secretive neighbor with pink satin handcuffs.

She relaxed by the creek, the setting sun highlighting the greens of the trees around her and her animals. It was truly a unique spot which she was so grateful to have. She couldn't imagine living in those town houses with people so close on either side. She appreciated this creek, with the wide open spaces, a ready path, and a spot for the animals. And maybe all because of the creek she'd ended up finding a solution to so many cold cases. She certainly came here to find joy. She knew the media would hound her as she helped to solve each case, and that usually meant her front yard would be out of bounds again. Most of the time the media didn't follow her to the backyard, but she couldn't guarantee they wouldn't.

She didn't even want to contemplate how many cold cases this last case would close. At least she hoped Annette Helmsman's deathbed confession should help close several of them. And now with Steve's involvement confirmed, that would be another matter resolved, if not two. And potentially a lot more.

Once the authorities got digging into that stuff and checked out Steve's finances, who knew how many other women were paid to stay quiet? Doreen wondered if some of those women were still alive. Maybe they were buried on his property. Not to mention, who was the body they found burned to a crisp that they had first thought was Steve? On that note, she walked back to the house where she called Mack.

His voice was exhausted as he said, "Please, not tonight."

She winced. "I was just making sure you were okay," she improvised. "I know it was a pretty rough day."

"You think? On the other hand, Steve is in jail, locked up, and not saying a whole lot. But now we have reasonable access to everything in his life. It'll take weeks to run it all down."

"Unless you get more from him," she said. "You might want to play the Penny card with that. I'm pretty sure he might have had something to do with the deaths of George and the nurse."

"In what way?"

"I just feel like Penny and Steve have been friends, if not more than friends, for decades. And I think that was the source of the fighting between her and George. He was probably always worried something more than friendship existed between them."

"Interesting line of thought," Mack said. "We can use that. We can interview each of them and see what the other has to offer."

"Of course, if it's true love, neither will roll on the other."

He gave a half snort. "True love tends to fall by the way-side for self-preservation when it comes to jail time."

"They're both getting jail time regardless," she said. "But what we can't have is reasonable doubt that Penny worked alone, and then Steve walks free on yet more crimes. Or both being involved and not proving either case clearly. Of course, if he's already going away for several murders …"

"Depends. We don't have a full investigation going yet at Steve's house. We'll return to his property, probably with cadaver dogs. Then we'll see what we can find."

"So whose dead body was that who burned in the fire at Steve's house?"

"Police business, Doreen." He sighed. "We're checking into it."

"Good," she said.

"You sound exhausted too," he said.

"With good reason," she retorted.

"If you would stay out of trouble for once …"

She snorted. "Absolutely! Wouldn't that be nice?" Then she smiled and said, "I'll see you tomorrow, if we're still on for dinner?"

"We are. Not to worry."

"Great," she said. "In that case, I'll hang up. I'm sitting by the creek, trying to relax and unwind. I need a good night's sleep tonight."

"You need several good nights' sleep, and you need to stay out of trouble."

"With all the antiques gone, and pretty much everything else resolved with Penny and now with Steve locked up, I think I should be good to go. Oh, except for one thing."

"One thing?" His voice turned dark when he asked.

"I did find something oddly incidental."

Mack gave a heavy sigh on the other end. "I don't like the sound of that. What? Where?"

"Well, it will give you a good laugh when I tell you," she said. "I did find handcuffs. Not in the hydrangeas but in a patch of heather."

"Still an *H*," he said, chuckling. "And why would you have found handcuffs?"

"I took the rest of the dirt back to my neighbor. And, while I was there, I saw something shiny in his big heather patch. They were just so full of beautiful blooms that I had to admire them. And then I saw the metal object. When I pulled apart the heather to take a closer look, I realized what was there. So I used a stick to pull them out."

"Handcuffs?" he asked in disbelief.

"Handcuffs in the heather at my neighbor's house, yes," she said, laughing. "So, you should be happy it's not at my place."

"I highly doubt they're significant in any case, so that's great. I bet your neighbor loved it."

"So not," she said. "In this case, they're not real handcuffs either."

And she knew her humor should have been a dead giveaway, but Mack was obviously tired when he asked suspiciously, "What do you mean, *not real?*"

"They're wrapped in pink satin," she said with a giggle.

He snorted and then chuckled on the other end. "Well, I'm glad to hear that."

"And, of course, they're quite dirty, as if they've been there for a while. I do have them here, but I'll just toss them in the garbage." She didn't plan on doing that, but she wanted to hear if Mack had any reason she shouldn't.

"You do that," he said. "I'm pretty sure you don't need

anything else on your plate right now. Anyway, I've got to go. It's been a rough day." And he hung up.

She hung up too. Then she picked up the handcuffs and put them in a ziplock baggie with the paper towel she had lain them on and set them on the nearby bookshelf that was already fairly stuffed again. She frowned at that, but she didn't really have any other place to keep the handcuffs. It wasn't like she had a cupboard where she could store evidence. She did have a couple spare plastic baskets though. She went into the hall closet, pulled out the stack of baskets, and put the cuffs in the top one. Then she put it away again into the front closet. She called the animals to her for an early bedtime, and they all trooped upstairs.

Chapter 3

Saturday Early Morning ...

THE NEXT MORNING, Doreen opened her eyes. The first thing that popped into her head was spaghetti. Today was spaghetti day, and she couldn't wait. Her stomach already growled, and she wasn't even sure if she'd eaten last night. Probably just a few crackers with cheese. She did that most days, and the days morphed into each other. Yet her stomach had gotten used to having some regular food, cooked by Mack, but last night she'd been too tired and too exhausted to do much. The day's events had caught up with her, making her beyond aware of what she'd been through, and all the things she still had to do as well.

She still lay in bed, plotting her day and sensing where her three pets were. Goliath was curled around her head. Mugs lay across her feet. She thought she heard the tiny squeak of the nearby overhead perch for Thaddeus. Her body tried to convince her not to do more. It warned her that she'd pay if she moved.

She shook her head and said, "You should have a hard day of work in your own garden today." She shifted and gasped in pain. But then she remembered the fight with

Steve and that garden work she had done at Millicent's on Friday, followed by all her own backyard gardening accomplished yesterday and realized she had every right to be sore. She slowly made her way out of bed and into the shower.

However, Mugs's barking caught her attention. She stepped out, wrapped herself in a towel, and asked, "Mugs, what's the matter?"

He ignored her and kept barking. Then she heard somebody at the front door. Groaning, she wrapped a bathrobe around her and raced down the stairs. She peered through the living room window to see Mack standing there with a glare on his face. She sighed, disarmed the security, and opened the front door.

"And what's the bee in your bonnet?" she asked.

"Me?" He looked at her in surprise. "It's early still, and you already look angry."

"My body is sore from yesterday, and I just got out of bed and into the shower."

"Good. I'll put on the coffee while you finish up and get dressed."

She rolled her eyes at him, then returned upstairs as he headed to the kitchen. She really should make him buy his own coffee to refill her stock, but, the fact of the matter was, she probably still owed him for many meals. So really a pound of coffee wasn't a hardship.

Dressed and with her hair brushed back but hanging damp around her shoulders, she made her way downstairs.

Mack looked at her and said, "You're still tired. And have you lost more weight?"

"I don't know," she said softly. "My pants are a bit looser."

He shook his head. "Did you eat at all yesterday?"

"Didn't we have sandwiches together?"

He nodded. "Did you have dinner?"

She frowned and shook her head. "I think I had a few crackers with cheese."

He sighed and brought out a frying pan, then opened her fridge.

"I don't have any ham," she said, "but I do have cheese." She watched with interest as he put toast on and then added butter in the pan and proceeded to crack a full half-dozen eggs. She frowned. "Didn't you eat?"

"This is for you," he said in a dark voice. "You have to eat."

When the eggs were almost done, he picked up the cheese and grated it over the top, then worked it into the soft egg mixture. At the end he sprinkled a handful of chives from her garden into the eggs. She stared at it in fascination and said, "You just made that out of nothing."

"That?" He smiled. "I made it out of eggs and cheese. Isn't that amazing? Scrambled cheesy eggs made out of eggs and cheese."

She glared at him. "You don't need to be sarcastic."

"No," he said. "I don't." He put the scrambled eggs onto a plate, grabbed the toast from the toaster, buttered it, and plated everything before setting it on the table. "Now, eat."

"I can't eat all that." She gasped. "That's six eggs!"

He glared at her and said, "I'll finish what you don't eat if Mugs and Goliath don't."

She sat down as he put a cup of coffee in front of her too. She smiled and murmured to her critters, "He might have arrived grumpy and angry, but I'm quite happy to have something different to eat."

"What do you mean, *something different to eat?*"

"I was getting a tiny bit tired of cheese and crackers."

He stared at her plate for a long moment. "Have you made anything else for your breakfast?"

"An omelet. Have you showed me how to make anything else?" she asked, forking up her first bite of scrambled egg. She stopped, closed her eyes, and sighed in delight. Several more moments went by as she inhaled half of her plate.

Mack shook his head. "We only made you a plain omelet. And you've done that on your own. I have the pictures on my phone you sent me as proof. I didn't show you how to add things to the omelet or how to take the eggs and just make some simple scrambled eggs, like this."

She nodded. "This wasn't simple."

"It's very simple. You saw me make it."

"Sure, but it doesn't have a simple taste. It's deep and rich with flavor and cheese." She ate like a starving woman because, at this moment, that was what she was. Before she knew it, only a little bit of scrambled eggs were left. She scraped it onto her toast, lifted the toast, and polished off the first piece. Then she sat back with a happy sigh but looked at the second piece of toast and said, "I don't think I can eat it."

"I highly suggest you try." Mack walked over to the cupboard and brought out the peanut butter and jam.

Doreen slathered both on and cut the bread in half. She gave him half and then started on the other. He picked up his half and ate it in three bites. She watched it disappear while she nibbled on hers.

"That's the problem with you," he said. "You put so much effort into your eating, you've burned up all the calories before it hits your stomach."

She ignored his comment and ate as slowly as she wanted. Then she picked up her coffee and asked, "So what's got you so upset this morning?"

"Where are they?"

She frowned at him in confusion. "Where are what?"

He growled, "The pink satin handcuffs."

She looked at him and tried hard not to smirk but couldn't stop it. Her lips twitched, and the first snort of a giggle escaped. And then she burst out in laughter. Mack glared at her. And Mugs, who had been quietly sitting at Doreen's feet, jumped onto his back legs and woofed at her. She smiled but was still laughing helplessly as she reached down and cuddled him close. And then she heard an even odder sound. She looked over at Thaddeus perched on the windowsill, imitating her laughter. It was the weirdest cackling yet snuffling sound she'd ever heard.

At that, Mack burst out chuckling.

"Wow, we're all just a mess this morning," Doreen said, still giggling. She looked at Mack and asked, "Why do you care about the handcuffs? You were all for me throwing them in the garbage last night."

"I want to see them," he said.

Snickering, but happy to go along with his request, she hopped to her feet and walked to the front closet. She pulled out the stack of baskets and brought the top one back, so Mack could see the bag with the handcuffs in it.

He lifted it up and said, "You put it on the paper towel?"

She nodded. "And then I put the paper towel in the bag, in case anything fell off."

He nodded and carefully looked at the handcuffs still inside the plastic bag.

She refilled their coffee cups, then sat, noting the resigned look on his face. She peered at the bag in his hand, but it was hard to see from her position. Plus the lighting was wrong. "What do you see?"

"Initials *MP*," he said. His voice was heavy and deep.

"Initials? What?" She jumped to her feet to look closer. "So, we can return them to somebody. Do you really think they'd want them back?"

"We can't return them to anybody," he said quietly. "Because I'm pretty sure these handcuffs belong to a woman, a known prostitute in this town, but one who disappeared about ten years ago."

Doreen stared at him for a long time. "But the handcuffs couldn't have been buried there for ten years."

"No, I suspect not. The material would have rotted away."

"So …"

"So, we actually had a problem with nonessential evidence from the case disappearing from the station."

Her jaw dropped. "From the evidence locker or whatever you use to keep all that stuff in?"

Mack nodded. "In cold cases, we don't throw everything away. Some police detachments do when they run out of storage. But obviously, if we're still trying to solve a case, we don't get rid of the various pieces of evidence we have."

"But this is hardly pertinent evidence, is it?"

"No, it was taken during the investigation, and it didn't have any fingerprints or anything on it, and her purse was found in the alley, nearby where she was known to work. Everything was photographed, and the digital copies were kept," he said. "But the purse and the contents went into an evidence box."

"But you didn't have anybody to return it to, so what

happened to it?"

He shrugged. "It was kept with forensic evidence for a long time. And then this stuff disappeared. We assumed at the time it had been tossed and no one marked it down. The cleanout was official so no one was really upset ..."

She stared at him in fascination. "So you don't think this is relevant to the cold case on her disappearance, which is probably a murder, but you are thinking it might be related to whoever broke into the storage or the evidence locker or whatever you want to call it."

He nodded slowly. "Exactly."

"So, let me get this straight. A woman's presumably murdered, and you collect all kinds of items for forensics. But, after testing, whatever is of no interest, you have nobody to give it back to because she has no family. So you hang on to the stuff until the theft of the stuff. What ... How many years ago?"

"Seven," he said slowly. "In this case."

"So, years after the original disappearance, but I'm calling it a murder, somebody dumps the box—which does seem to point the finger at somebody in the police department. At least initially. But maybe then the dumpster was raided, and I'm thinking kids got to it and threw it away here in the neighbor's yard. And yet it wasn't important to the case, so the kids stealing it shouldn't have been important to the case either. More nuisance value. Likely someone pilfered the purse, hoping something worth money was inside, but, not finding anything, they just threw everything away."

He nodded. "But then where is the purse? Or, in this case, the rest of the box?"

"That could be anywhere. Particularly if the purse was nice. The rest? ... Possibly tossed in the bushes as they walked or drove by. ... That part we're not likely to ever know. And it ends up at my neighbor's front garden," she said. "See? That says *prank* to me. Was anyone who worked at the force related to Richard? Maybe even hated him? Or, like I said first, it could have been just some curious kids ..."

"Of course it could," Mack said. "And, more to the point, it ends up in your hands."

She chuckled. "Is there any way to know what else went missing?"

"The items weren't considered pertinent for the case. That entire box disappeared."

"But you had a list of these items somewhere, right?"

Mack shrugged. "We're checking into that."

"And, if she was a prostitute, and this is related ... You know? Like the pink satin handcuffs, was the rest of the evidence similar paraphernalia?"

He nodded. "Yes, definitely. From what I remember."

"So maybe somebody knew the box was there and just wanted to have some fun with it?" she asked cautiously, not sure how to put it.

"Most people don't steal sex toys from a police evidence room. Nor try out used sex toys."

"No," she said. "But obviously something happened. Was other stuff taken as well?"

"No. And the box wasn't important to the missing person's case—yes, now considered a murder after so long—so no one cared until it went missing. Even then it wasn't a big deal, just chafed for my friend."

"So this box could have been targeted but why? More likely it was tossed and no one wanted to get into trouble so stayed quiet. Someone saw the box in the garbage and snagged it without knowing what was in it ..." she pondered that.

"And that's why people did know about it," he said. "After three years had passed from the original missing person's statement, we reopened that cold case, trying to find anything new we'd missed. It was decided that the box contents were of no value. And that box was put aside."

"So, if the box was stolen shortly after the department's review of the box, that makes it sound targeted to me. But"—she shrugged—"it's a theft of unimportant items, and that's unpleasant, but that doesn't mean it was necessarily criminal."

"Well, it's criminal *because* it's theft," he said in a dry tone. "Especially when stolen from a police department. But the originating case file is obviously not at the top of any of our pending files to work on."

"That's very interesting," she said. "Still it feels like the items were just tossed away. As if someone had this stuff and just threw it out a window as they drove by. Then, considering that, in all those years—seven since the box went missing—wouldn't the satin have deteriorated somewhat more?"

"How close to the house were they? Were the heathers protecting them? Where are the sprinklers? Or were the handcuffs just sitting there under the heather branches, dry and protected? Is there any reason they wouldn't have looked weather-beaten or old by now? I'll take them to forensics and see if they find anything on them."

"Be my guest," she said.

He nodded. "So, when we're done with our coffee, you'll show me where you found them."

She rolled her eyes. "Sure. My neighbor'll love that."

The good thing was Richard didn't even show his face.

He was probably too embarrassed. Doreen walked over with Mack and showed him exactly where she'd found them. No pink satin remnants were anywhere around the heather.

"You should take a bunch of photos, I guess," she said. "But I never thought to when I pulled them up. There's where the chain between the two of them was or whatever you want to call that piece that connects to the handcuffs. You can see it was dug in slightly."

Mack nodded and took several photos, then said, "Good. I'll take these and the handcuffs into the station and see what the chief wants to do."

"Sounds good," Doreen said. She stood outside while he drove away, Mugs and Goliath sitting at her side. Both watched Mack, whereas Thaddeus apparently showed a great deal of interest in the heather. He plunked up a stem and tossed it on the ground and went after another one and then another one.

"Oh, no you don't," she said. "We don't ravish plants as pretty as this. Particularly when they're not ours." She scooped him up gently onto her hand and placed him on her shoulder. He squawked in outrage and tried to get back to the heather, but she didn't let him. Back at the house again, she closed the front door and cleaned the kitchen. She was at odds and ends.

With the Steve scenario in police hands now, and, still not sure what to do with the six hope chest boxes she'd found above the front closet, she was tempted to start in on the Bob Small newspaper clippings, but suddenly she was really tired. Deeply tired. Maybe she was tired of humanity acting like this. Humans really were a lousy species to be the supposed king of this planet. Maybe a coffee would help. And, of course, with Mack coming and going, they were running out of coffee. Just as she went to put on some, Nan called.

"How about a cup of tea and a croissant?" Nan asked.

"Well, tea, yes, but I'm pretty stuffed. I had a very big breakfast."

"Lovely," Nan said. "If you come down, you can take the croissants back for lunch. They're full of ham and cheese."

Doreen brightened. "That sounds wonderful!"

"You must be exhausted," Nan said. "Maybe I should come up to you."

Caught by that idea, Doreen chuckled and said, "If you would like to come for a walk, sure. Do you want me to pick you up?"

"No, no, no," Nan said. "I'm walking outside to my patio now. I'll be there in fifteen minutes. Put on the tea."

Chapter 4

Saturday Morning...

L AUGHING IN DELIGHT, Doreen knew it was too early to
put on the kettle, so she'd wait a few more minutes to
give Nan time to walk over. With her gang, she headed back
to the creek, where she watched the water during the early
morning hours. She was becoming addicted to the sound of
the creek as it rippled gently along the rocks. It was rising
again but not by much. Maybe a couple inches. It was
enough though to make her stop and look at it sideways.

Then she stared back at her property. The house had
been here for a long time, but it hadn't occurred to her that,
in the case of flooding river conditions, the water might run
into her basement. At that thought, she needed to talk to
Nan about it. As she turned to look for Nan, Doreen saw her
grandmother on the other end of the path. With the animals
in tow, Doreen walked to meet her halfway, carrying
Goliath, while Thaddeus perched on her shoulder, and Mugs
walked with a bounce in his step. Nan immediately cooed to
each animal in turn, giving them all hugs and pats and words
of love.

"Nan, do you ever get water in the basement?" Doreen

asked as soon as they reached her.

"Not really," Nan said. "We have once or twice over the years, but it depends on how bad the melting snowcap season is. Nothing bad in decades. I did worry about the furniture down there, but thankfully that's all gone."

"You don't have sump pumps, do you?"

Nan shook her head. "No, I don't. Just keep an eye on it."

"But you stored all those antiques down there," Doreen said, struck by the magnitude of that catastrophe, if it had come to pass. "What if they had been damaged?"

Nan shrugged. "Thankfully it didn't come to that. Most of those were collected in the last ten years. If the river rises too fast, as it comes down your creek, it soaks up in the surrounding ground. That's why the houses are as far away from the river as they are. It's still a foolish idea to have a basement when you're along a waterway like this because it's not actually the river flooding that can hurt you. It's groundwater accumulation. It might be something you want to look at though."

"Look at what?"

"Adding a sump pump. You have the ones outside the house, in case you hadn't found them yet."

When Doreen didn't respond, Nan looked at her and said, "Oh, dear, I haven't explained about that, have I?"

Doreen shook her head slowly. "Outside the house?"

"Two of them, in fact," Nan said. "It stops the water from going into the basement."

"But you said it did flood several times?"

"Only if the sumps aren't working. Back then I didn't have those. They were added in later." They walked into the backyard, and Nan headed to the corner of the garage, moved some of the bushes back, then pointed at a round wooden lid. "Lift that up," she said.

Doreen did and was shocked to find a metal cylinder and some mechanical device inside.

"Now, hoses should be around here somewhere," Nan said, turning around. "You hook a hose onto that end and take it all the way down to the creek."

"But that's a long distance. What kind of hose do you hook to that?"

Nan wandered around the outside of the house. "There was a box here."

Then Doreen remembered, under the heavy growth at the side of the house, she had found a low-lying box, maybe a wooden version of an irrigation box. She told Nan, and they headed there. Nan opened it, and inside was a black-and-blue pump hose. She came back out with one end and said, "Take the other end of this and just unroll it down to the creek. They are quite heavy."

Even with the warning, Doreen was surprised by the weight of them. "Do we need to do it now?" Doreen asked.

"If you look where the pump is," Nan said, "you'll see there's a little water already in the cistern."

Doreen backed the hose down the lawn. When she returned, Nan gave her a shorter hose.

"Go connect this one to that one," Nan said. "These simple clamp-lock things are on the end."

Doreen did that, snapping the locks together. Feeling better about that, she rejoined Nan again who was ready to show Doreen how to attach the elongated hose to the pump. Nan popped it in the tube in the ground so it was connected to the device inside, and then she said, "Get a hose, dear." Doreen looked down at the sump-pump hose, and Nan shook her head with a laugh. "The garden hose."

It was just around the back of the house where the porch was, so Doreen brought the end of it to Nan.

"Turn it on," Nan said. "And direct the water into this metal cylinder."

Doreen watched and heard the pump making a weird sound while being filled with water. And then it sent water shooting all the way down the much bigger hose to the creek.

"Perfect. That's how you keep the water out of the basement," Nan said. "For now, just leave this in place. We can tuck the sump pump hose up against the fence. You have another fifteen to twenty feet of that hose in the box. If you connect a longer one along the fence, it will drain over the path into the creek." Nan bustled around to the low, flat box and pulled out another set of hoses. "Back over here where the police dug up my garden," Nan said in a mild outrage, "there was another sump pump."

Doreen frowned and hurried over to the far corner. "I don't remember seeing one." But, sure enough, where the policemen had turned over the garden and had dumped a pile of dirt was another circular wooden piece in the ground. "And I just thought that was garbage," Doreen said.

With Nan's help, they scraped all the dirt off the top and lifted that circle. And there, beneath, was another metal ring and a pump. They repeated the process of hooking up the sump pump hose to the pump itself.

Then Nan said, "Now you can leave these out, and any-time the water starts to rise, these two pumps will keep the water out of the house. Although, if you landscape back here, you should consider burying permanent pipes in the ground, so you never have to worry about these hoses again."

Doreen looked down in the hole and realized the pumps

were at least four feet deep in the soil. That was probably pretty close to where the basement was. But if they were permanent ... She nodded and said, "So, as long as we keep these pumps running, no water will go into the house, correct?"

"Correct," Nan said with a smile. "It's always an adventure living by the water, dear."

Doreen sighed. "You know what? It never even occurred to me to ask you about these, since I didn't know they existed. I just noticed the creek was rising, and that's what had me worried today."

"I hear you there," Nan said. "Hopefully I would have remembered before you flooded."

Doreen shuddered. "But I'm good to go now, right?"

"You are," Nan said.

Doreen smiled, grateful she'd thought to ask Nan. "I've been watching the creek rise for the last week," she said. "And I started to wonder, just how high could it go?"

"You can expect it to rise almost flush with the hill here," Nan said. "But it doesn't last. We might even only see it for six to eight hours. Yet something you should take a moment and look at. Every once in a while, we get these heavy floods, and then you could have trouble with the pumps."

"Right," Doreen said, staring down at the pump nearest her in the corner. "Hopefully not this year."

"Hopefully not," Nan said comfortably. Then she looked around. "Did you put on the teakettle?"

Doreen chuckled. "No, but I will. Come on inside, Nan."

Chapter 5

Saturday Morning ...

INSIDE SHE MADE tea and sat down with Nan.

"So, bring me up to date," Nan demanded. "You didn't give me all the details about Steve."

"I gave you a bunch of the details," Doreen said with a grimace. "And you can't really blame me for not giving you all of that. He did attack me once again."

"And I had to hear it from Darren, who told Richie, who came to tell me."

Doreen sighed. "I didn't want you worrying. Another attack from yet another criminal wasn't something I wanted you to deal with."

"It's timing, dear," Nan said. "I need times."

"It's all about the bets for you, isn't it?" Doreen groaned.

"At this point, it's also about cold cases, and I gather the police have a lot to work on now."

"Lots of leads to follow, threads to tie up, people to interview, et cetera," Doreen admitted. "Steve was heavily involved in a lot of different things. And, of course, the cops are thinking maybe they'll find those women he supposedly paid off are buried on his land."

Nan looked thrilled, and Doreen rolled her eyes. "You might want to consider the fact that those women lost their lives because Steve was greedy."

"Yes, but just think," Nan said. "That's three missing women. Just think of the families who have been waiting to hear about their loved ones."

"They were all vulnerable women. Who knows if the families are even aware they went missing," Doreen said quietly. "We have to remember the humanity in all this inhumanity."

"Of course, my dear," Nan said, but she looked even more thrilled. "I'm so happy you're doing this. Obviously it's very helpful for everyone. Not to mention people all across the country. Who knows how widespread this could go?"

"Mack said something about taking police cadaver dogs to Steve's property. Hopefully they find something."

Nan brightened at that too. She would literally glow if she brightened up more than she already was. "How exciting. It would be fascinating to figure out how those dogs operate."

Doreen thought about it and nodded. "You're right. I'd love to see them work."

"Call Mack, my dear," Nan said. "Maybe he wouldn't mind if you watched."

"I'm pretty sure he *would* mind," Doreen said, laughing. "He wasn't happy with me this morning as it was."

Nan's face twisted into a curious but knowing look. "This morning?" she asked delicately.

"He stomped over here mad," Doreen explained. "Made me breakfast and then wanted to know about the handcuffs I found."

Nan clapped her hands together and bounced in her

seat.

Doreen smiled. "You get more excited and act like a teenager every day."

"It's my right," Nan said with an airy hand wave. "You've heard about adults going into their second childhood. I've just stopped at the teenage years. It's such fun. When I was a teenager, I couldn't do anything. I mean, *nothing*. But now? Wow." She leaned forward and said in a low voice, "Tell me about the handcuffs."

"Only if you don't share it with the rest of your buddies at Rosemoor," Doreen said with a warning.

Nan drew a cross over her heart. Doreen wasn't sure if that was good enough, so she reiterated, "Promise me, Nan."

Nan glared at her, and then her shoulders slumped. "Fine." But then, when she heard all the details, she laughed, trying to hold it back behind her hand as she giggled. "Oh my," she said. "Are you sure they don't belong to our neighbor?"

"He appeared to be quite offended," Doreen said. "And he didn't come out when I showed Mack where I found them."

"I think I remember something about that missing woman, presumed murdered," Nan said. "There was a big outrage about getting the women on the streets some help, so they could find another way to make a living. One of those hot topics that come and go. You know how, this year, we'll worry about women who are prostitutes because life and circumstances forced them to sell their bodies. Then next year, it's all about the drug dealers and the addicts who keep the drug dealers in business. Then it will be single moms and abusive relationships." She shook her head. "I know we need to help them all, but it just seems like they fade in and out of the news and don't get steady attention."

"And, of course, that's basically what happened here too," Doreen said, "because the case went cold."

"Another cold case," Nan breezed through the statement as if she expected it.

"No, not really. I'm not looking into it. The handcuffs were in a box the police were getting rid of because the items didn't contribute to the case."

"Maybe," Nan said, nodding her head. "And yet maybe not because now you've found the handcuffs, so who knows?"

Doreen nodded. "I'm not going there. Let's just put it that way."

The two women then relaxed and had their tea. Nan perked up, lifted her pointer finger, then reached into her pocket and said, "I forgot about these."

And, sure enough, she had two ham and cheese croissants. "Nan, you must have very big pockets," Doreen said in admiration. "Nice going." In truth, she wore a big afghan-style brightly colored sweater with those big square pockets on either side.

"It's perfect for this," Nan said. "And you were going to show me those diamond earrings. You forgot last time."

"Oh my." Doreen hopped to her feet, went up to her bedroom, then brought down the big bowl holding everything she'd found in Nan's clothing. "Take a look at this," she said. "I put everything in here."

While Nan was a bundle of excited energy and looked through the bowl, Doreen couldn't stop thinking about the police canines. She decided to call Mack. And, ignoring his growl, she asked, "Is there any chance I can watch how the police dogs work?"

"I don't know," he said, sounding surprised. "I'm planning on being there. If I can get away. By the way, forensics didn't find anything usable on the handcuffs."

"Oh," she said momentarily distracted. "Okay, that's too bad."

"It's what I expected."

"Right, back to Steve's property. I guess I'm asking if I can be there too," she said hurriedly. "Obviously I won't get in the way." He snorted at that, so she said, "Okay, let me amend that. I'll try not to be in the way."

"For all I know, it's almost over," he said. "I'm late as it is."

She sighed. "Oh, well, let me know then if you find anything." Then she hung up.

Meanwhile, Nan looked at the big bowl full of coins, rolled bills, and business cards. She dug around in it and smiled. "Who'd have thought I lost all this stuff all those years ago?"

"I hardly think it was lost as much as misplaced or just left as is," Doreen said. She rummaged in the bowl herself and found the earrings. She picked them up and handed them to Nan.

Nan got a soft look on her face as she sat back and said, "These are real diamonds, you know?"

Doreen hated the fact that immediately her thoughts swept to the money value of them, when, in truth, they were pretty earrings that she would wear herself.

"You probably wouldn't get a whole lot for them," Nan said. "They're in an old-fashioned setting."

She handed one to Doreen, who stared at the multiple hearts inside. "The style looks timeless to me."

"Keep them," Nan urged.

"They mean something to you," Doreen said. "Who did they come from?"

Nan just gave a little finger flutter and said, "A friend."

"Another lover?" Doreen asked drily. "You did quite well with them in terms of gifts, didn't you?"

"I did, indeed," Nan said, her hand holding the bowlful of money. "Have you counted how much money is here?"

"Not yet. I started off trying to keep track, and then I just gave up."

"You'll have to buy some of those wrappers for the coins. A lot of money in coins is here."

"I know. I don't think I can just take it loose to the bank."

Nan shook her head. "You can't do that, but you can get a few coin wrappers from the dollar store or from the bank and roll them up yourself." She pulled out the larger bills and straightened them, so they could be laid flat. And then she looked around, grabbed an empty chair, put the bowl lower, and said, "Let's sort through the money, and we'll see if anything else is in all this."

With Nan's help, they sorted out the hundreds, the fifties, the twenties, the tens, and the fives into separate stacks. They even found a couple older bills no longer used in Canada.

Nan tapped them and said, "You can still take those to the bank."

"Any point in keeping them?"

Nan shook her head. "Only as a curiosity."

With the dollar bills sorted, they pulled out all the business cards and the little pieces of paper. Doreen handed all of those to Nan to read through. The business cards, once reviewed, Nan just tossed into the garbage and said, "Whoever they were, it was a long time ago. So nobody there of interest." The notes were read next. She smiled and said, "Well, this is a grocery list, and this is a list of errands, like to go to the bank and to the post office." She crumpled and threw them away. "Thank you for the trip down memory lane."

Then they sorted through the coins, stacking up the bigger ones and then all the way down until only pennies were left in the bowl. "And these, you can't really use anymore either," Nan said. "I think, if you roll them, you can cash them in at the bank though."

"Okay, so I have to go to bank first to get the rollers, then go back to the bank—after I roll the coins."

"You might as well take a lot of these dollar bills and deposit it in the bank too," Nan said. "You've had so many break-ins, you're just lucky nobody stole this bowl."

Doreen stared at her. "I didn't even think of that. How much money is here?"

"Let's find out," Nan said and counted each stack, with Doreen noting each pile's total on a notepad. With all the bills laid out in front of them, they added up to a grand total of $924.

"Nan, that's huge!"

"Good," Nan said. "Add in the coins, and you'll find you're up to one grand. I don't think you'll hit a thousand dollars for sure, but you won't be too far off either."

"Wow," Doreen said, getting up and pouring more tea. "Oh, and a couple weird little things are in the bottom of the bowl here too." She pulled out what looked like a marble and handed it to Nan. "I don't have a clue what that is. We did find three in the Ming vase though, or maybe two." At that she found herself looking around, wondering what happened to them. And then she said, "And a bunch of these little colored rocks."

"I vaguely remember these," Nan said, rolling the wooden ball in her hand. Only then her gaze caught on the *colored rocks* and was immediately distracted. "These are opals, dear. Unset opals." She picked up one to turn it in the light watching the pretty colors shine from inside the stone.

"I thought they were really pretty," Doreen said. Then she frowned. "You know what? You'd think I would recognize the opals. I used to have good jewelry."

"But opals are only for some people's taste. Your ex-husband was all about diamonds."

"True," Doreen said, as she studied the opals, letting the sun hit them and watching the fire shine through. "What do I do with these?"

"When you have a little bit of money, get them set into something," Nan said. "They were from my grandmother."

Doreen gazed at Nan. "Just like the pearls and the emeralds?"

"Exactly," Nan said. "And the cufflinks. It's amazing just how much of that was kept, and I didn't even know it. But the emerald necklace? That was unique." Then Nan frowned. "Can I see them?"

Doreen went upstairs, took the velvet pouches she'd found in the hidden drawers in the antique bedroom set, and came back down. On the kitchen table, she pulled out the pearls, the beautiful emerald necklace, and the cuff links.

"Absolutely beautiful," Nan said. "If you need the money, sell them. But, if you don't, you might want to keep them. They're heirlooms. And you need to keep them safe, in case you get broken into again."

"Hopefully the security system will hinder that. Plus

word has surely gotten out that all the antiques are at Christie's now." Doreen gently stroked the green gems. "They're beautiful," Doreen said. "I'll never have a place to wear them though."

"You don't know that," Nan said. "And I'm not telling you to keep them. I'm letting you know that you *can sell them*, if you want, but, if you get enough money from all the other stuff, maybe you won't need to."

"I guess selling jewelry isn't quite the same thing as selling antique furniture, is it?"

"No," Nan said, "but, if you found a good jeweler, he might sell them for you. He would probably buy them off you, clean them up, and maybe fix some of the broken settings, if there are any, and then sell them himself."

"At a much higher cost," Doreen said drily. "I could ask Scott first."

"Yes," Nan said. "But then, if you think about it, he's doing you a service too because he's buying them from you."

"I have to admit I'm hesitant to sell any of these," Doreen said.

"Good. You're allowed to be sentimental," Nan said. "You do need to get an insurance appraisal done and get them covered. Because, if they ever do go missing, the insurance company will pay you for them."

Doreen nodded, grabbed the notepad with her to-do list, and wrote that down. "I suppose I should get the insurance looked at now that the house is empty too, shouldn't I?"

"You should," Nan said. "Definitely you should. And thank you, by the way, for taking care of the other paperwork. You got it all digitized because I got the email as well." Nan looked around at the bookshelf and smiled.

"I still have those four books though," Doreen said,

looking at them.

"Ask Fen Gunderson," Nan said. "He might know somebody who's interested in them. Otherwise, just give them away, my dear. They're like the last little bit of leftovers, so why not?"

"Except for the six hope chest boxes."

"What do you want to do with those?"

"I didn't find any living family members who cared to have it, except to sell the stuff, and that didn't really feel right. We have a historical society in town. I was wondering about taking them there. All the nightclothes were obviously hand-stitched and might be of interest. Then I'll see if they'd be interested in having some of the other items. And honestly I was thinking—and I mentioned it to Mack—that maybe I'd like to keep the sets of dishes."

Doreen paused, then continued, "I should find out from Scott to confirm they aren't massively priceless items." She said the last phrase in a mocking tone. "But, if they're not, and if it's not something he wants, I thought maybe I would keep the dishes and put them to use. I only have your broken dishes, as it is."

"Everybody needs a good set of Sunday china," Nan said in delight. "And I'm pretty sure the woman who owned the hope chest items stored in those boxes would be happy to hear you were keeping them."

"It's three boxes full of dishes. And I thought maybe the love letters could go on display along with the nightdresses and other clothes."

Nan tapped the table as she stared off in the distance. "I think I remember hearing about somebody involved in the memorial society, but I can't remember who."

"I need to make some phone calls and maybe stop by

with a few items to see if they're interested. Obviously we have the Pioneer Society here, intent on preserving our history, and maybe this history is important too."

"Yes," Nan said. "I really like that idea. So you also have all of Solomon's files he'd collected throughout his life as a journalist, and that's about it?"

"And the Bob Small newspaper clippings I kept from your friend," Doreen said with a smile.

"Very true," Nan said. Then she hopped to her feet. "I'll let you go now. You might want to casually walk past Steve's house and see if the police dogs are working now."

"I don't want to get involved in anything official," Doreen said. "I've pissed off enough people in the law enforcement community."

"You've also delighted many people, some in the law enforcement community as well. You shouldn't feel bad if you want to know how the police dogs work. I'm sure there'll be a crowd anyway." Nan paused, then looked at the creek and back at Doreen. "Maybe you should go from the creekside."

"I also wanted to do some gardening."

On that note, the women stood and went to the back-yard, where Doreen pointed out how far she'd made it with the digging and the weeding.

"This is starting to look really nice," Nan said. "And remember to keep an eye on those pumps."

With a wave, Nan headed down the creek. Doreen didn't feel comfortable leaving her to walk all on her own, but there wasn't any reason to follow her either. So she stood in place until her grandmother disappeared around the corner. It really was just a couple blocks back to her place. With Mugs and Goliath at her feet, Doreen smiled and said,

"What about a walk in the other direction?" Mugs gave a bark, while Goliath gave a meow.

And Thaddeus, not to be outdone, said, "Thaddeus is here. Thaddeus is here."

"I know, big guy," Doreen said. "And, if you promise not to laugh at me anymore, you can ride on my shoulder."

He started to laugh. Not quite as creepily and not quite as loudly but it was the same type of snicker. She shook her head at him. "You should mind your manners," she said as she led the way toward Steve's property.

"You should mind your manners," Thaddeus said. "You should mind your manners."

Doreen groaned. "How come you always imitate the wrong things?"

Thaddeus ignored her at that point, shaking his wings and ruffling up his feathers, as if to get comfortable on her right shoulder. She smiled and walked along the river. She'd had enough to eat from Mack's visit this morning, and she really was good for hours. Besides, she wanted to see what police cadaver dogs could do. As she walked up to the river though, she found several cops lined all around the property. And there was Arnold.

He lifted his finger in her direction and shook it.

She glared at him. "I'm allowed to walk here."

"You are," he said, "but you're not allowed on the property."

"I wasn't going on the property," she said. "I just wanted to see the police dogs. See how well they worked."

"A little too well," he said grimly. Then he pointed to several markers on the lawn.

She frowned. "Please tell me those aren't all bodies."

"Then I won't," he said and turned his back on her,

leaving her in silence.

"Wait, wait," she said. "Are they?"

He glared at her and said, "Do you have any idea how much paperwork we have to do now?"

She smiled at him, knowing by now it was just his gruff exterior. "Do you understand how many families might find some closure now?" she asked.

He gave a clipped nod and said, "I do, but we don't need you here right now. We got this."

Chapter 6

Saturday Early Afternoon ...

DOREEN DIDN'T WANT to go, but, with the cops not allowing her to take pictures, to explore, or to do anything but stand mutely nearby, she finally turned away and headed home. The animals were happy to stay or to go. They were just happy to be out again, as if her one day of rest had been more than enough for them, and they were ready to zip ahead and to do things. She wasn't sure how that worked, but, considering the somberness of what was happening here at Steve's house, she was glad to know these women—if those were actually bodies—would finally get a chance to be heard and to have their families notified. Still, it was a very sad business.

Her steps slowed, stopping to pick up rocks in the creek, which was definitely rising. She studied the other rocks to find almost none were left visible in the middle of the river, and the water now rose onto the bank. As she stopped and studied the water height, she realized that quite possibly, within another few days to a week, she wouldn't be able to walk along the banks, meaning she'd lose that path up to Steve's place. She wondered if she had rubber boots anywhere. That would allow her to still walk a little bit here, even if muddy or flooded somewhat. But then, paths went along both sides of the river too, so she could keep tabs on what was going on at Steve's place before the water rose enough to cause her any concern. Worst case scenario was she'd have to walk on the street side of the property.

Finally back home again, Doreen walked inside and made coffee and grabbed one of the two croissants, then sat outside on a chair by the veranda table. She needed to work on her garden, so, as soon as she was done eating, she bounced back to her feet, walked past a small clump of heather and giggled. She immediately looked at the neighbor's house, considering the pink satin handcuffs, and couldn't think of a less likely pairing. Under what circumstances would a pair of sex-toy handcuffs end up in the heather patch of his garden?

They could obviously have been thrown there, maybe even before he moved in, depending on when he bought the place. She didn't know how long he'd been in that house. And that meant, chances were, the handcuffs weren't his, but somebody else had dropped them. But why here? And how? Another prostitute? Although how she'd have gotten her hands on them while in police possession, Doreen didn't know.

No, her best bet was that some kid had swiped the box from the station and went through the stuff, tossing what was of no value. Hell, it could have been several kids, divvying up the contents of the box. But how did a kid get by the police to steal evidence from their possession?

All these thoughts ran through her head, but she didn't have any answers. It was frustrating because she could do just so much if she had no further clues. Not the least of which was more info on the original cold case. Mack hadn't said much about that case. With her mind coming up with more and more crazy ideas, she kept working away in her garden, getting yet another full bed done, then worked for another hour as she tossed out some of her initial ideas.

Maybe the original thief had his goods stolen too. That would be justice. The new person could have been walking or driving in the area and seen that their haul was useless and had thrown them into Richard's garden bed. Although why there, she didn't know. Still it wasn't like Richard was ever into gardening and likely wouldn't have found the items but for her. She'd never seen him do anything more than stand in that doorway, like an ogre. Still, that didn't mean he wasn't out there in the dark with a flashlight when she wasn't around. She giggled again at that image because he was so not the kind.

But then she was making a judgment call, and that wasn't fair either. When she needed a break from her hard work, she stopped, wiped the sweat off her forehead, and sagged back. Maybe this was enough for today. She'd done an extra ten feet. That didn't seem like very much, and, in a garden that had been well-kept, it wouldn't have been. But, for here, where the plants needed trimming and the roots needed some loosening and the weeds and the entire ground around it needed turning over, it was definitely a lot.

She really should get some topsoil back here. But not until she had an idea of what she was keeping and what she wasn't keeping. She had a little room around the side of her house for that to be delivered, but she didn't think she could get anything like a dump truck this far back to deliver those huge cubic bags of topsoil that far, so she could wheelbarrow the bags farther. But that looked like a ton of work too.

Unless they had a crane that could lift it over the house.

She brightened at that idea and then realized somebody probably did, but there would be a high price tag to go with it. She walked back into the house and decided on having some fresh lemonade. She'd had enough coffee for a while. She hadn't had fresh lemonade in a long time, but she'd also never made it herself.

"How hard could it be?" she said out loud to Thaddeus. She sliced fresh lemons, dropped them in the pitcher, and filled it with cold water and ice cubes. Then she grabbed the sugar and put in one-quarter cup. She stirred and then tasted it. It was ever-so-slightly sweet water. Shaking her head, she grabbed more lemons, squeezed them, and gave Thaddeus one of the halves. Thaddeus busied himself, pecking away at it.

Changing her mind about the bird's treat, she snagged it out from under his claws when he wasn't looking. Then she gave him a piece of celery instead. "Remember green," she said to him. "Green is healthy for you. I have no clue about yellow."

He shot her a look, then pecked on the celery. That was all good. She tried the lemonade again. "Okay," she said. "It's now supersour." She added a bit more sugar but judiciously. She didn't have much, and she wasn't a big sugar person anyway. At least she didn't think so. But every time she was down at Nan's, she managed to gobble zucchini bread or something equally delicious. So, maybe her taste buds were changing. She tasted her lemonade again and smacked her lips.

"Perfect," she cried out. She poured herself a tall glass, put the pitcher in the fridge, and stepped back outside to her garden. She studied the small patch where her heather was in beautiful bloom and said, "You know what? Heather is always gorgeous at this time of year. But there's so little of you that it's not enough to make an impact."

The shrubbery had spread over time. She really needed to have ten times more and wondered if she could potentially ask her neighbor for some because his garden was seriously overgrown. His would do better if she took out about half of it. But where would she put some?

She wandered down to the edge of the garden where the creek was and considered how the heather would help to retain the soil when the river rose and fell again, depending on the height of the water. Plus some heather would make a really nice border along that edge, now that the ratty old fencing had been torn down. She went over to her garden, dug some up, and moved the heather toward the creek. Then, not giving herself a chance to think more about it, she grabbed her shovel and walked around to the front to her neighbor's house. She pounded on the door. At least, she pounded the third time when the first couple times didn't do any good.

Finally the door opened, and Richard glared at her.

She gave him a beamingly happy smile. "I was wondering if I could have some of your heather. It's really overgrown and could use a bit of thinning out."

His eyebrows shot up to his forehead, then he glared at her some more. "Why? So you can find more things in it?"

Her jaw dropped. "Oh, I never thought about that," she said, taking a few steps over to look at the massive heather patch. "What else would you have in there?"

"Nothing," he said. He looked at the heather and shrugged. "I guess you can have a bit. But I don't want it to look like you stole any."

"I wouldn't be stealing now, would I?" she said gently. "You said I could have it. Therefore, I'd just be moving some of it."

His brows drew together as he upped the wattage of his glare.

She smiled and said, "I don't know if you have more in the backyard that you want to get rid of, but I was thinking to put some along the creek edge. Nan's backyard has suffered when she wasn't able to look after it quite so well. So, I'm trying to bring in a few more plants to help revitalize it."

He looked at his heather and then pointed to where it had bowed out into a big clump in the front.

From the color alone, Doreen could tell it was a different variety entirely.

"Why not take some of that one? It's a different shade, which doesn't really fit."

She nodded. "That would give your patch a more uniform look." She walked into the middle of his rocky bed area, bent down to where the odd-colored heather was, and said, "If you don't want this one, I can probably pull out most of it, and then these two behind it will grow together. I can probably even shift them over a little. Or move some of your ground-cover rocks to hide the hole."

He nodded. "Just make it look like you've not taken a big lump out of the middle."

Doreen nodded. "I can do that."

Before she even finished her sentence, he was back in his house. She moved the rocks away gently. And, with a great deal of difficulty, figured out where the heather started and stopped. At least, in terms of that one color. With that separated, she gently got her shovel underneath and loosened up a clump. By the time she was done, she had a clump that was a good two feet across.

Richard wouldn't particularly like that because that would leave him with a big hole. She walked back to her house, grabbed a wheelbarrow, came back, and then lifted the loosened heather into the wheelbarrow. Afterward, she gently loosened and shifted the other plants over a few inches at a time.

Now, with it all replanted and the flowers nicely arranged, it hid most of the hole. She piled up the rocks again and grabbed the hose and rinsed off the rocks, just to make it look like nobody had been here. As she curled up the hose afterward, she found Richard nearby, his hands on his hips, studying her work.

"Sorry," she said. "I didn't know if I should've asked to use the hose, but I was just trying to clean up the mess from digging and transplanting everything."

"It looks good," he said grudgingly.

Pleased, she smiled at him. "The plants were fairly crowded, so they'll do better now."

"I thought heather liked being crowded."

"It does," she said cheerfully, "if it has space to go. But it's all up against the rhododendrons here, so they all fight for nutrients. With that overhang from the roof, they aren't getting enough rainwater either."

"I was looking at doing some underground irrigation, but well ..." He shrugged.

Doreen understood. Whether it was time, money, or energy, everybody had a reason not to do something. "Looks fine as it is," she said. "The heather won't be in bloom for too much longer, so it's nice to enjoy them while they're showing so much color."

He nodded, and she gave him a smile and grabbed her wheelbarrow, then slowly walked back to her yard. She wished she knew what else he had in his backyard. Maybe she could ask for a few more plants. She almost wanted to laugh at her superthrifty ways, but gardeners were gardeners. Although she'd managed to talk to a few when she was married, it was useless talking to most society women about it because they didn't do their own gardening.

Whereas here she was hoping to meet with some plant lovers and maybe exchange some plants. She had a couple daylilies, but they were the standard ones, and she knew some massive ones were nicely colored out there. Same with the dahlias. She'd love to have some of those dinner plate dahlias she had seen on her walks. They were gorgeous. And Penny's dahlias were probably pretty. If Doreen could get a couple of those, that would be lovely too. But then she knew she was persona non grata with Penny in jail right now, so it didn't matter how nicely Doreen asked. She wouldn't get any.

She wondered whether she should check in the local paper or online for any plant-swap groups. And she had to consider if she had anything to swap. A lot of Nan's garden was overgrown, but some sections were seriously suffering.

She headed to the edge of the creek and transplanted the heather along the far left corner of the fence. It would give a really colorful edge to the bank there. With that done, she dumped the rest of the loose dirt around it, packed it in tight, walked to the creek with her shovel and scooped up some fresh water and poured it all around the newly transplanted heather. She repeated that a few times until the plants were nicely soaked. Finally she stood here and admired her work. "I know you'll struggle for a bit," she murmured to the plants, "but that's okay. You'll be fine soon."

Then she pushed her wheelbarrow to the garage. When she came out the side door, she saw a vehicle pulling in. It was Mack, coming over to cook dinner. As soon as he hopped out, Mugs almost trampled over Goliath to get to Mack. Goliath meowed in anger and took off in the opposite direction. Doreen laughed. Maybe that had been Mugs's plan all along.

She glanced around and found Thaddeus had walked with her into the garage and was even now at her feet, looking up at Mack. Although her bird was a good size, he was still low to the ground, and she had always worried about him getting trampled. It was one thing for Mugs to send Goliath tumbling into somersaults, but it was another thing entirely for poor Thaddeus. She scooped him up and put him on her shoulder.

He got all excited, ruffling his feathers and crying out, "Mack is here. Mack is here."

Mack looked at him and said, "Looks like Thaddeus is here. Thaddeus is here."

Thaddeus opened his mouth and echoed him. "Thaddeus is here. Thaddeus is here."

Doreen shook her head. "Please don't encourage him."

Mack chuckled, gave Mugs a hug and a cuddle. "He's great," he said, slowly standing up to rub his hand along Thaddeus's head. Then he looked around and said, "What happened to Goliath?"

"Mugs happened," Doreen said. "He sent Goliath into a series of somersaults, and Goliath took off because he was offended." Doreen looked around and called out, "Goliath! Come on over here, buddy." But there was no answer. She glanced at the neighbor's house and found the cat sitting right in the middle of the heather. Thankfully a different spot than the one she'd disturbed today. She winced. "Goliath, come on, buddy. Get off of there."

"I guess that neighbor is not terribly friendly, is he?"

"He surprised me today," she said. "I asked him if I could have a piece of heather from his garden for my back garden. He let me take out this huge section that was an odd color. He didn't like that shade, as it turned out. He wanted the heathers in a uniform color, so I was allowed to take that one. But then I had to move and shuffle a bunch of the others in his bed, so it used up the newly created space. It looks pretty good now, but Goliath is sitting just off to the left of where I had been working."

As she said that, she walked to the edge of the driveway and called him, but Goliath wasn't having anything to do with her. Instead, he stretched out, full length, on the carpet of purple. "No, no, no," she cried out. She ran up the driveway and reached down to snag him. Just before she got to him, he darted toward Mack.

But that was enough for her to see what he had disturbed. She frowned. She'd worked in this garden bed earlier for at least a half hour, but not in this section. This big solid clump Goliath had lain on had something else shiny in it. She carefully parted the heather and found a ring. She hooked it with another little twig and lifted it, carrying it to Mack. She held it up and said, "You can blame this one on Goliath, not me."

He looked at it with raised eyebrows and said, "That's a pretty fancy ring but doesn't look valuable."

She nodded. "And it's just a bit away from where the handcuffs were."

He glared at her, and she shrugged.

Just then, the neighbor's door opened behind them, and the neighbor stepped out. "Now what did you find?" he growled.

Doreen gave him the sweetest smile. "A ring," she said. "I figured it must go along with the handcuffs."

His face turned beet red, and he stepped inside and slammed the door on her.

She chuckled. "He's afraid I think the handcuffs were his. Thinking that he might have invited over an escort."

Mack looked at her in all seriousness. "But we don't know that he didn't, do we?"

She shook her head. "Nope, we sure don't. But any escort wouldn't likely have been carrying these, if they came from the police station. So, do you want this, or am I giving it back to my neighbor?"

"Let me get a baggie for it," Mack said, the fatigue heavy in his voice.

"I'm sorry. I guess I've dumped an awful lot of work onto your plate lately, haven't I?"

"You have," he admitted. "But also a huge sense of getting something accomplished, so I don't mind. None of us do."

"I went to watch the dogs sniffing at Steve's place, but I wasn't allowed on the property," she complained.

"I was told you were there," he said. "Nothing was allowed to distract the dogs. I didn't think of that when you asked."

"Oh, I wasn't thinking of that either."

"No, I'm sure you weren't. The problem is, the dogs did find something, several somethings. But we have to dig very carefully."

"I'm sorry," she said quietly. "I saw the markers on the lawn."

He nodded. "That doesn't mean it's necessarily cadavers. No jumping to conclusions in that case."

"When can you get in and dig?"

"They're at it now. If we do locate any human remains, then, of course, we'll have to investigate further, in a big way."

Doreen nodded. "But still, if it's human remains, it'll be very nice to know these people have been found and recovered."

"We're not to that point yet," he said and asked, "Coffee?"

"Sure. Or you can have lemonade."

At that, he looked at her and asked, "You made lemonade?"

Chapter 7

Saturday Afternoon ...

DOREEN SNIFFED AT Mack's shock and drew herself up to her full height, wrapping her mantle of disdain around her, and said, "It's not hard to make. It's just lemons and sugar water."

His lips twitched, but he said meekly, "I'd love to try a glass of lemonade."

So she pulled out the pitcher from the fridge and poured him a glass. And then she waited, hating the expectation that it would be awful to his taste buds.

But he looked surprised. "This is good."

"Don't sound quite so shocked," she said drily.

He chuckled. "Pleasantly surprised. You're getting better."

"I've hardly cooked anything. You're the one cooking."

"Which is why we'll eat spaghetti tonight," he said, "but you're making it, not me."

She put the lemonade back into the fridge. "What do I need to get started?"

He stood beside her and said, "Pull out the ground meat, the celery, and the onions. The garlic is on the counter already. We'll need fresh tomatoes too. Do you have any of that red wine left?"

She shook her head. "I don't think so. It would be vinegar by now if I did."

"Good point," he said. He got out the big pot, and, per his instructions, she learned to brown the ground beef, add in the onions, the celery, and all the spices. And then finally the chopped fresh tomato. .

He grabbed two spoons, gave one to Doreen, and he dipped his in the sauce. "*Mmm.*"

She was hesitant but sampled her sauce. "It's good," she exclaimed.

"Of course. Now we'll let that simmer," he said.

She sniffed the top of the pot and said, "Wow. I really hope I can remember this."

And then he pointed at his phone.

She looked at it and said with a big grin, "You videotaped this, didn't you?"

He laughed. "I did, and I can send it to you. You can have it for the next time you're making sauce."

"I would make pots and pots of this and freeze it all, so I have food for weeks."

"There's no reason not to, except for the fact that you don't have much freezer space."

She looked back at the pot and sighed happily. "You're right. And I certainly can't afford to do this all the time ..."

"It's a very cheap meal," he said in all seriousness. "You can afford to eat this at least once a week, if not three times."

Just then her stomach growled. He glared at her. She raised her hands defensively and said, "I ate earlier, but then I've done several hours of gardening since." She motioned outside, so she could show him how far she'd gotten.

He looked at it in surprise. "It's starting to look really good."

"I'm a long way from being done though. I'm still trying to make sense of what's in the garden. Once I've done this side, I have to start on the other. And, if I want to make a complete change in design, I need to put that down on paper."

"What kind of change?"

She motioned at the tiny deck and said, "I was hoping to bring that deck all the way out here, so it will be about twelve feet across. It'd be nice to have a little barbecue and a place to sit at a bigger table for a meal, not just that little tiny bistro set."

He nodded and said, "That wouldn't be hard. Especially if you kept it under two feet high. You wouldn't need permits."

At the sound of *permits*, her stomach sank. "Permits sound expensive."

"They can be, and it also depends how far back the house is from the riparian zone."

Her heart sank even more. "Meaning?"

"Meaning, you might not do anything without a permit too close to the creek. I think the rule is fifty feet, or maybe fifteen meters." He frowned. "I'll have to double-check." He walked down to the creek by the property line and used his stride as a measure, then walked forward. He stopped about twenty feet from the house. "You know what? I think you could probably bring a deck addition almost up this far."

She looked at the large space in surprise.

"Really. And there's no reason not to if you want some-thing that big. Although you don't really need to have it this big. Still no basement windows are underneath that would be blocked, so we could make it a solid deck with a nice set of stairs coming down off to the side. You could have a patio down here too."

She looked at how far he had walked. It was almost to where she had finished her weeding. "We don't have to bring it out as far as the fence either," she said, studying Richard's fence.

"No, you need six-foot clearance for that without asking for a variance, and there's really no need. We could put stairs down on that side too, so you could get to the flowers, if you wanted. As a matter of fact, it would take a nice chunk of the garden out of here that you wouldn't have to worry about." He turned around, looked, and said, "By the time you brought some topsoil in here and got this area sorted out, you could have a nice lawn garden on both sides and a big deck."

"I'd love a big deck," she said warmly. "Something with that lovely outdoor furniture—lounges, chairs, and a table."

"If that's the case, maybe twenty feet isn't too far out. That is big though, and you have to count in the fact that the bigger you make it, the more money it will cost."

She winced. "It's the labor as much as anything." Then she stopped and said hesitantly, "I was wondering if it was something I could do."

He looked at her in surprise. "It's not that it's hard," he said cautiously, "but you have to get things level, and you've got to dig in your patio blocks. You know? Those concrete anchors? You've got to put all the beams in, and that's not hard, but it does take a bit of work, as they are heavy. I'd be more concerned you might not be able to lift the wood."

"Oh. And, if I can't do that, I can't lift those big concrete blocks either?"

"The blocks aren't bad. It's the wood, and it depends if we'll put like four-by-fours all the way from one end to the other," he said. "I think the biggest length we can get away with is twelve feet, without paying delivery, but that doesn't mean we can't do doubles."

"Right," Doreen said, as if she understood. "I'll have to look it up. But I really like the idea of a big deck."

"I can see that. You spend a lot of time out here, so why not? It's not like you'll ever have a pool because of the creek, but you can certainly have a patio and a nice deck—even an outdoor kitchen, depending on how much money you want to spend."

Her jaw dropped at that. "An outdoor kitchen?"

He nodded enthusiastically. "Barbecue, counter, sinks. They're really nice."

She nodded slowly. "Did you consider the fact I already have one kitchen which I don't know how to use, so a second kitchen I don't know how to use is kind of redundant?"

He spun on his heels to look at her, then burst out laughing.

She glared at him. "I'm really not happy you come here to get your daily dose of humor. I mean, I guess the internet's pretty boring for you now." Inside, she was tickled though because she had meant it as a joke. And he had taken it that way.

"Oh, you're great," he said, as he swung an arm around her shoulders and tucked her up close against his chest, giving her a hug. "Besides you are learning to cook. You're the one who made that spaghetti sauce today."

She thought about that, and a pleased smile crept to her lips. "You're right there," she said. "But a barbecue seems like it's even more dangerous than that electric devil inside."

He still chuckled as he shook his head and said, "Some people would say barbecues are easier. I love barbecuing."

"Really?"

"Really," he said. "I know you probably have some maintenance you need to do on the house, but, whenever you sort out the money from the antique sale, you might want to consider doing something like bringing in a gas line and putting in a natural gas stove or barbecue out here. It's easy enough to add a couple counters on either side and some cover overhead. You don't have to get too fancy, but I think that bathroom in the downstairs is right beside here, so it'd be nothing to bring out a sink. You'd have to redirect the wastewater into the sewer line."

She kept nodding, as if she knew what he was talking about. In theory, she did, and the more she got caught up in his excitement, the more she could see the deck and how much potential it had. "How hard is it to pour concrete?" she asked.

That stopped him cold. He winced. "It's not *hard*," he said slowly.

She glared at him. "But we're back to the same problem, where I might not be able to lift the bags?"

He considered that and said, "Honestly you probably could, and you could probably mix it yourself, but you couldn't spread very much at one time, and concrete is kind of fussy that way. But there are molds you can buy or maybe even borrow, where you can fill one mold at a time, if that's the speed you can work by yourself. You could even then have something like flagstones going all the way down to the creek and through the garden, depending on what you want."

She nodded. "It would be a lot cheaper to do it myself. You know how much it'll cost to pay somebody?"

"It will cost a lot," he admitted. "But first you need a plan—and don't cut your plans short just because you're thinking you can't do it all yourself. I might be able to come and help do some of the more physical lifting." Then he paused and moved around, studying the space in question.

"We can also bring in a cement truck, if we have all the foundation work done and the patio framed out already. It'll be a fairly clean and smooth patio and walkway. That won't be quite the same look though, and we do have to pay the truck to come. But then they can pour from your driveway here." At that, he motioned with his arms to the side of the garage. "You know what? You could pour a sidewalk all the way down to the front of the garage, so you don't have all this nasty mess to deal with in here too."

Doreen looked at the *nasty mess* where half gravel, half weeds existed, where things were growing and taking over.

"Potentially," Mack continued, "we can *somewhat* pour it down near the creek as well. You can repair the pathway in the water areas. You can't add new ones without permits though."

"So ... because a broken sidewalk is there, we can pour a new one?"

Mack nodded. "Exactly. You can't add something new to a riparian zone, but you can fix what's already there."

She walked down a few feet, studying the broken pieces, and then said, "So what I should do is sit down with a piece of paper, draw something up that includes a large deck, the patio, and the pathways, then clean out this old mess because we can't pour on top of all that. I'm not sure how we frame circle pathways."

"It's not so much circles as much as curves," he corrected absentmindedly. "But you could have a path that meanders, or you could have a path that goes through the gardens and comes back to the center, or you could just have a nice path that goes right from here to the creek. That's where you walk the most anyway, isn't it?"

She nodded and said, "And then just keep the gardens on either side as they are. And have a nice grassy spot on either side of the sidewalk. That would be pretty and elegant."

"It would be very simple. Adding the patio up here and a deck on top, I think you have a really nice space."

"What about a patio down at the far end of the riparian zone by the creek?"

"If something's there already," he said, "we could pour concrete. Otherwise, you'd just get some of those concrete patio blocks and put them on top of some of that gravel. That's not a problem."

She nodded. "Sounds good. I'll have to think about it." She walked back over and studied the deck. "Any idea what it would cost to build this deck addition?"

"Well, if you do it yourself ..."

"How about I do it *myself*," she said with emphasis, "but maybe with your help? I don't know if we could get anybody else to help for a day or two. It's one thing to pay for a day's labor versus getting somebody in who actually does it from scratch. The thing is, I don't know where to start."

"I've built a couple simple ones," Mack said. "And this is fairly simple because we're already almost at ground level, so we're just coming off the deck that's here. We don't have to worry about anything else but putting a railing on it, unless you want stairs all the way around so you can sit on them."

She loved the idea of that. "But that'll add more money too, won't it?"

He nodded. "Railings are not cheap, so that cost may counter the other cost."

She smiled. "You know what? I'm really liking this idea." She hopped up onto the little deck and already it felt claustrophobic. She walked back inside, and he followed. She noticed the ring on the table in a plastic bag. She picked it up. "You should put that into your pocket, so it doesn't get forgotten," she told Mack.

He took it from her, and his facial expression changed as he studied the ring.

"Are we thinking that's real?" Doreen asked.

He tried to hold it in the light, but it was seriously dirty. It looked like a solitaire diamond and one of some serious size, but it was almost too perfect.

"I think it's fake," she announced.

"I wonder," Mack said. "It will need a good cleaning."

"It's been washed many times," she said. "When you think about it, that garden has been watered time and time again."

He nodded and went over to the sink to put a little bit of water on the ring inside the bag, enough to rinse it. And then, he sealed the bag again. "I'm not sure if it is costume jewelry."

Doreen shook her head. "I think it is. But a good one. Like one someone wore and kept the real one locked up. So good enough to not have the *fake* of it be noticed. I'd say that's at least a carat in size." It was a not-too-contemporary setting with simple high sides and with a single diamond perched on the top. "That's a traditional engagement ring look. But the more I look at it, I can see how fake it is."

Mack looked at her, and she continued, "Look for an inscription. They're usually inscribed with something."

It took a bit to get the lighting just right because the band itself was fairly thin.

"What was the woman's name?" she asked, as she tried to look with him. "That's an *M* showing.'

"If it's who I think it was," he said, "her name was Meredith."

Chapter 8

Saturday Late Afternoon …

"IT LOOKS LIKE you've got something about to blow Meredith's case wide open," Doreen said, matching his quiet voice. "I don't know how that would have come off her finger."

"Well, it's off her finger, unless you found a finger over there," Mack asked, his voice thickening.

She shook her head. "No, but again I wasn't looking. The metal's glint in the sunlight caught my eye. And remember. Goliath showed us this one."

He nodded. "I may have to go over there and take a good look at his garden."

"You probably should," she said. "Now we've got hand-cuffs *and* a ring."

"I know," he said. "I'm not liking this at all."

"No, but it makes my neighbor's place a very interesting scene right now."

"Not so interesting," he said. "This stuff has probably been there for a long time." He looked over at the neighbor's house and frowned. "Any idea how long he's lived there?"

She shook her head but pulled out her phone and said,

"Nan will know."

He looked at her. "I can also check the property records."

She shrugged. She'd already dialed Nan. As soon as the voice on the other end called out cheerfully, Doreen said, "Good afternoon, Nan. Do you have any idea how long Richard has lived here?"

Nan, as if understanding this wasn't a joke but a more serious question, said thoughtfully, "You know? I'm thinking at least ten years."

"No longer than that?"

"I don't know. It's been quite a while." Nan's voice was apologetic, as if she knew that wasn't enough detail.

"That's all right," Doreen said. "I can find out with an internet search."

"Is it important?"

"Not too important," Doreen said warmly. "I can find it out on my own."

"Okay then," Nan said. "Are you okay?"

"I'm doing fine. I've been gardening and am about to sit down and have spaghetti."

"Oh, lovely. Does that mean Mack is there with you?" Nan asked in that gushing tone of voice.

"Yes," Doreen said with a chuckle. "I made the sauce as he hovered over me."

Mack spoke over her, saying, "She did just fine."

Nan sounded thrilled at Mack's voice. "Oh! I'm so happy, dear, so happy he's giving you cooking lessons."

"We were just discussing maybe putting a deck out in the back."

"Did something happen to it?" Nan asked, puzzled.

"No, no," Doreen said. "It is still there, but we're thinking of making a bigger one, where I can put couches or chairs and an umbrella for sitting outside in the sun. And maybe, you know, a barbecue."

"Oh, that would be lovely. Take some of that money you've been making and do something with it."

"That was the plan," Doreen said. "But it'll be quite a while before all that auction money is settled up, and I actually get a check. It depends if I can figure out how to make a deck happen before that with a lot less money."

"You sold those car parts," Nan said. "If you take that money and exchange it for a bigger deck out back, that's a perfect trade-off."

"Oh," Doreen said. "I wasn't even thinking about that, but it might be possible. It depends on the money situation. I haven't a clue how much the taxes are on this place, and that's coming up in a few months."

"Less than a few months," Nan said. "You should probably already have the paperwork. I think it's about five hundred dollars."

"Really? That's not too bad then," Doreen said. "I was expecting it to be about five thousand."

"Oh, maybe," Nan said. "Honestly I've forgotten." And then Nan hung up.

"That's not reassuring," Doreen said, turning to Mack. "Five hundred to five thousand dollars is a huge difference."

"But to Nan, it's only a zero," Mack said with a chuckle. "And you can find out your property taxes easily. There's a government website for that. You just put in your folio number for this place, and you're good."

"And I'll find that where?"

"Good point," he said. "In the paperwork from previous years."

"Oh, great," Doreen said. "I suppose the taxation was held back because of the change of ownership."

"That would make sense. But that's all right. You'll figure it out. And it shouldn't be that much. My taxes aren't all that much, and neither are my mom's."

"*All that much?*"

"Maybe six to seven hundred dollars," he said. "Start by figuring out what you want for a deck. Then we can work out what it would cost to get the materials and to do it ourselves because it's only a little bit off the ground. I don't think it'll be that much, maybe two thousand dollars."

She swallowed hard but nodded bravely. "*Only two thousand.* So, in theory, if I could pay the taxes and the other bills coming in with Nan's cash in the bowl and my gardening jobs, I could still use some of the money from the car parts to put in a bigger deck." At that, she stared outside and realized just how badly she wanted it.

Mack nodded. "For the existing deck, all you have to redo is the boards. And they're looking pretty old as it is, so you should take off these old boards, and we can slap some new ones down. You need the supports for the little roof over here, but you could take the railing off if you wanted it to match."

She loved the idea of that too. "Well, I guess the first thing to figure out is how many of those cinder blocks we need with the anchors to put on the big beams. I'll have to do some research."

"You do that," he said. Then he returned to the stove and said, "It's time for you to stir the sauce."

She lifted the lid, but he pulled her back and warned her about the steam. When it dissipated, she stirred the spaghetti sauce, and its aroma filled the room.

Mack, however, looked at the sauce critically and said, "It's a little thick."

"Is it?" she asked with worry. "What do we do then?"

"Well, water will distill down some of the flavor. Do you have more tomatoes? Tomato soup, crushed tomatoes, tomato sauce—anything that we can use to boost it?"

She led him to the cupboard with the food and said, "This is what there is."

"Right. I remember this from cleaning it out last week. You really don't have much, do you?"

She shook her head.

He nodded, went to the fridge, and pulled out five fresh tomatoes. He chopped them and added them.

"I guess it really doesn't matter, does it?" Doreen asked.

"Straight tomatoes can make it very strong," he said. "You can use tomato soup to cut some of that, if you want. You can also use a bit of cream." And, at that, he opened the fridge, found her cream and poured in a hefty dollop. She watched in amazement as the cream turned the sauce into an ever-so-slightly lighter color.

"So, now the tomatoes won't be so acidic?"

"You can also add sugar," he said, "but I'm not a big fan because it's too easy to ruin a good sauce."

"I don't like sugar anyway," she said.

"Unless it comes in the form of zucchini bread?"

She laughed. "Exactly."

Chapter 9

Saturday Late Afternoon …

"I WAS JUST thinking that this morning when I made the lemonade," Doreen said. "Because every time I go see Nan, she has either zucchini bread or muffins or something else yummy to come home with me."

"That's a good thing. She's looking after you."

"Sure," she said, "but shouldn't I be looking after her?"

Mack nodded. "And you are. You have to remember her mental state is what's really important right now. She has food. She has a roof over her head. She has money to spend—but what she really has now is a granddaughter who adores her. So, you keep doing you, and she'll keep doing what she does."

"I really like the sound of that," Doreen said quietly.

Just then Mack opened another cupboard, pulled out a big pot, and put it on the stove with a *bang*.

"What's that one for?"

"The noodles," he said.

She brightened. "What about the water?"

He nodded and said, "I put the teakettle on when you weren't looking."

She glanced at the kettle, and, sure enough, it was full of boiling water. He poured it into the pot and turned on the water; then he refilled the teakettle and turned it back on again.

"Does it make it faster this way?"

"Well, it's already boiled water, so it just has to heat up here because the pot itself has to heat up," he explained. "By then, we can add more boiling water, and we should have enough to cook the pasta."

"So, does that mean we'll eat soon?" Doreen asked in a woeful voice.

He chuckled. "Yes, it does. But it'll still be a few minutes, so we'll turn down the sauce and let those tomatoes cook. And then we'll leave the water here to boil, and I'll walk over to the neighbor's house to take a look at his heather."

She brightened.

He shook his head.

She frowned.

He laughed.

And she glared at him.

"Yes, I'm going alone," he said. "I want to make sure nothing else is over there."

"In that case, you should probably take my gardening gloves," she said, as she walked to the veranda railing and snagged the pair she had been using.

He looked at her and shook his head.

"Why? What's wrong with my gloves?" Then she looked down at them. "They're perfectly fine for me."

Mack took one of the gloves, slapped it up against his hand, and said, "This is why."

Doreen snickered. "It's not my fault you're oversized."

"I'm not oversized," he growled. "And, if I'm not allowed to make weight comments about you, then you're not allowed to make weight comments about me." And, with that, he spun on his heels and headed to the front door.

She wasn't sure if he was joking or if she'd offended him. She ran behind him and called out, "It's fine, you know."

At the door, he paused to look at her and asked, "What's fine?"

"Your weight."

He burst out laughing. "I know it is," he said. "And, besides, not everything that's oversized is wrong."

As soon as he said that, he winked at her and disappeared. She felt red-hot color wash up her neck and cheeks. And then she laughed because she'd asked for it by using that word. But still, with the animals trying to follow Mack, she was forced to stay inside because, as soon as she opened the door, all the animals would run over to the house next door. And she already knew that was a no-go. The neighbor didn't like her to begin with. And he didn't like her animals either.

She watched through the living room window as Mack went outside, knocked on the neighbor's door, and had a short conversation with Richard. Mack then walked to the heather with Richard, who was almost wringing his hands, as if worried about what else could possibly be found. Or worried he'd be blamed.

Mack continued to talk to him, but the conversation was too quiet for her to hear, and that drove her crazy. Mack went through the brush carefully, trying not to disturb anything, and then finally straightened and smiled at Richard, who looked relieved. As Mack walked toward her, she returned to the kitchen, so it didn't look like she'd been waiting for him, and stirred the sauce again.

As soon as he walked inside, the animals were immediately all over him, as if he'd been gone for hours. He scooped up Goliath this time and carried him into the kitchen. Goliath was half perched on his shoulders with his big guttural engine engaged, as Mack checked on the sauce.

"So, you didn't find anything, huh?" Doreen asked.

"Nope," he said cheerfully. "Much to his and my relief."

"Won't matter," she said. "You already have the engagement ring."

"She was a hooker," Mack said briefly.

At that, Doreen rounded on him, her hands going to her hips. "She might have been a hooker, but that doesn't mean she couldn't fall in love, find a partner, and try for a better life."

"Hey, hey, hey, I didn't mean it that way."

"Yes, you did," she said mutinously.

He rolled his eyes at her, lifted the teakettle, and added all the boiling water to the pot. "Maybe I did," he said. "That was poor judgment on my part. She probably did want a different lifestyle."

"What you're also forgetting," she said, "is someone in a vulnerable lifestyle needs to work for money. She's hardly going to throw away a diamond ring."

"Maybe," Mack admitted. "But we have yet to know if it's real or not. I'll wait until I get that back from the office."

"So, you will reopen the case now, right?"

He gave a heavy sigh. "I don't really have much choice but to take a closer look." He replaced the lid on the pasta pot and then lifted it again and poured in a hefty amount of salt.

Doreen stared at him.

"We've been over this before," he said. "The salt is needed. None of the spaghetti I've cooked so far has tasted salty, has it?"

She shook her head. "No, you're right. I don't understand why, but that seems to be the way of it."

"Exactly, so no panicking."

She grinned. "When can we put in the pasta?"

"In a few minutes," he said. "Hungry?"

"Starving," she said, laughing. "And so are all the critters."

While she waited for the pasta to cook, she fed the animals. And then she stepped out on the deck and studied the little bit of a deck she had now. If she could get a bigger deck, she would really love that. She hopped off the side, mentally marking off how far she'd like it to go. She needed to go back inside. She didn't have a tape measure with her, but she wanted at least twelve feet added to her little deck, which would make it probably seventeen feet total, so then another three feet would be even better. She took a large step and turned to face it, then nodded. She saw Mack by the doorway and said, "I do think twenty feet might be good."

"Twenty feet is big," Mack said. "We'll have to measure it off and put up some sticks or something for you to visualize it better. So you can figure out if it's too big."

"Meaning it would dominate the backyard?"

"Yes," he said. "You still want things to look proportionate."

"Right. In that case, sixteen is probably not bad."

"After dinner we'll check," he said. "If I don't get called into work again, which I have been every day this week, we'll take out the tape measure and put some sticks in the ground, so you can think about it."

She beamed at that idea. "The spaghetti will be at least

ten minutes …"

He rolled his eyes at her and said, "Hang on."

Then he must have gone into the garage because she could hear the doors opening and closing, and then he came out with the tape measure. Together, they measured off sixteen feet, which was pretty close to where she had estimated. He had a little stick in his hand. He used the hammer to pound it into the ground, and then they put one on the other side too. "Now if you take these two straight back to the house," he said, "that's sixteen by sixteen feet. And that's pretty big."

She nodded. "But if we put stairs down this side or a stairway there, this could be a patio." Then she motioned at the rest of the space, which would be close to another sixteen feet.

He measured it off, nodded, and said, "This is about fifteen. But if we attach the sidewalk on the side, which needs to be three feet minimum, that'll be eighteen feet and that leaves you the three to four feet for the garden."

"That works out quite nicely."

Mack went to the garden, picked up some rocks, and laid out what they were looking at. Every rock he placed down, Mugs came to sniff, and Goliath hopped from one to the other, following the line. Thaddeus supervised Mack the whole time. It was a real family affair.

"Now," Mack said, "the pasta should be done. Let's eat."

She laughed. "I'm more than ready. But now I'm really excited about doing something for myself too."

"You should be," Mack said. "You've done a lot for other people. Remember. It's all about balance. So, think about what you want, and then we'll figure out what it would cost to do what you think is best."

Chapter 10

Sunday Morning…

THE NEXT MORNING, Doreen rolled over, disturbing Goliath, who ran off. Then she groaned, closed her eyes, and willed herself to go back to sleep. But Mugs wasn't having anything to do with it. He wandered up on her bed—still just mattresses on the floor—snuffling into her neck and shoulder, and then nudging her with his head. "Really?" she mumbled. "Surely it's not morning yet."

"Thaddeus is here. Thaddeus is here."

"Sure you are," she muttered.

Mugs nudged her shoulder once, twice, and then reached out with one of those thick paws of his and dropped it on her arm. She winced at the roughness. "We'll have to get some cream for those pads of yours," she whispered.

She opened her eyes, looked around the room, and noted sunlight inside. So, whether she thought it was morning or not, the rest of the world seemed to think so. And certainly Mugs too. She rolled over on her back and reached out to scratch him, but he wasn't looking for that. He was looking to go outside because he woofed at her several times and then nudged her.

Groaning, she dragged herself vertical and made a quick trip to the bathroom. Then she led him downstairs. She disarmed the security and opened the back door, still yawning and still dressed in her pajamas, and let him out. She watched as he headed to the first bush and peed all over it. She groaned. "You know those peonies will never survive if you keep doing that, right?"

He ignored her and proceeded to tear into some of the grass right beside it as he dug several times. And then he dashed around, as if rejuvenated by an early morning spring air infusion. "I'll do the same," she said wryly. "As soon as I get coffee."

She let the door fall closed with him outside and went to put on the coffee. As soon as it was set to drip, she stepped onto the deck and stretched. She really needed to get back into yoga. Somewhere in the last few months, she'd lost that sense of calm and peacefulness that she had used to maintain her stability in that ugly relationship she had called a marriage. She looked around and realized just how much she wanted that bigger deck to add to her sense of zen.

She took several steps in the direction of the expansion and thought about how it would open up the yard completely. She could do stairs all the way around, or she could do railings on part of it. Both were just such great options. Thaddeus hopped onto a corner rock and fluttered out his wings.

Doreen figured it would make the complexity that much worse if she did anything other than right angle corners on the edges. She also didn't want to do something like that because complexity usually meant upping the cost. She went right to the edge where she could peer around the side of the house and thought about what her options were for that strip.

By the time the coffee was done dripping, she had a notepad, and she sat at the outside table, sketching ideas. She'd have to look up some photos online.

The problem with that was then she tended to want more and more. Just because everybody else had something grandiose didn't mean she could afford the same thing. And sometimes, simple was just the nicest. If she did it all in beautiful wood, she knew she'd have to treat the wood, but she wasn't sure how often. Ten years, maybe? And that depended, she thought, on if she bought pretreated wood for the decking, which would up the cost again but would help to protect the wood from the elements.

Her first cup of coffee disappeared without her even tasting it, while the second cup went down slower. And finally she walked to the creek with her third cup, the animals at her side, and turned to look back at the house. Mack had brought up an interesting point about proportion, and she understood that. She could have an outdoor couch. Maybe she could find something secondhand or even cheap at an end-of-season clearance too? Or maybe they could build a bench.

She frowned at that because really, at times, she wanted something soft and not superhard to sit on. She gave a happy sigh, wondering how much of it was really possible. The fact that Mack offered to help was huge because he really did have the strength she didn't have. She could get an order of the blocks delivered and pay the extra delivery fee, which she was hoping was only about fifty dollars. She could move the blocks in a wheelbarrow to the backyard, but she didn't think she could move the big six-by-six foundation frames, if they were using them. Maybe four-by-fours were all that would be required, but she wasn't sure if she could drag those around or not.

This was one of the few times when she realized what an inconvenience it was to be female. With that deck expansion in her mind, she made a few more notes and adjusted the rocks a little so she could get a better layout and get more artistic as to what she could have as a garden along the edges. She thought she wanted something that would give her a bit of shade for the deck, but she didn't want to block her view of the creek, so that might not work.

Humming to herself, she stepped back inside, looking for food. Then she remembered the spaghetti from last night. Chortling, she headed to the fridge and pulled out some leftover cold noodles and the pot with the leftover sauce. She warmed them in the microwave and then scooped some of the sauce from the pot and placed it atop the pasta.

With hot spaghetti on her plate, she sat back at her little veranda table and nodded, thinking about how beautiful it would be to have a full-size table out here. Instead of devouring her breakfast, she slowly ate it and enjoyed every bite.

She didn't have a copy of the video of how she had made this last night yet, but, while she sat there, she jotted down as many notes as she could remember about what she had done. She still had the notes and the video she'd created when he had made it the first time, but this time it had all been different because she had been the one creating the sauce.

And it was a sauce she planned on making over and over again. She didn't even want to freeze the leftovers. She just wanted to eat it all up. It was so good. After a lifetime or what seemed like not having much pasta, she was thoroughly enjoying having the simple white carbs again.

She laughed at that because her soon-to-be-ex-husband had watched her waistline for her all the time. He would probably approve of the fact she was bordering on scrawny now. In fact, Mack was constantly trying to feed her, and maybe that was a good thing too. But then she was gaining muscles. She looked at her arms and grinned because just that bit of gardening she had done since moving here had given her some muscle definition. Instead of the smooth and skinny arms she used to have, she now had some nice hills and valleys. Gentle ones, of course, but still more definition than she'd ever seen in her life.

While she ate, she studied her neighbor's house and wondered about the ring and the handcuffs. Although she knew Mack had gone into Richard's garden and had looked for whatever else might be there, she wondered if he'd missed something. Hell, she wondered if she'd missed something too. She'd been the one who was in there, moving things around. It was definitely disturbing to think two items had been there. More so that one was so much more sentimental, while one was so little. And yet, maybe both were indicative of this Meredith's split life. Maybe she was engaged. Maybe she had found her way out, and the handcuffs were a reminder of what she still was in her mind.

Doreen sighed with a slow shake of her head. She couldn't imagine a lifestyle like that. And, once again, she was forever grateful to Nan for giving Doreen a roof over her head and a massive amount of very expensive antiques inside, underneath that roof.

As she relaxed back and looked around her backyard, she realized she didn't have any plans for the day. So, maybe she should start off with some research. She didn't want to get sidetracked with gardening sites, but she knew, as long as she had her own computer, that would happen.

And what about Meredith? Doreen grabbed her phone and sent Mack a text, saying she'd just had spaghetti for breakfast, and it was delicious, then asked him what Meredith's last name was. He sent back a **Good morning** text and left it at that.

She glared at her phone and typed a swift response. **And the last name?**

Why?

Because I want to do some research. Since my research has ended up helping everyone …

Meredith Pollock.

She chuckled when the name came back immediately. "Dear Mack," she said to herself. "You might not like all the paperwork, but you definitely like closing cases."

And, of course, a prostitute was one of those more vulnerable cases, where the public wanted to believe the police didn't give her the same attention as they would have somebody prominent in society. And maybe there was some truth to that, but she also thought it had a lot to do with the lifestyle. It was easier to get information from one corner of society than it was the other. Doreen would likely run into the same problem herself.

She moved to her laptop and started researching. Almost nothing was there to be found, just an odd mention in a cold case folder online on a website she had never seen before. It listed Meredith as a missing person. Doreen paused. A missing person or a murdered person? She wondered at that. She texted Mack again, asking if they ever found a body.

Nope.

She nodded but didn't reply and then kept going. With her trusty notepad nearby, she wrote down Meredith

Pollock's name on the edge and started taking notes. But, as soon as she put the notepad down, she wondered ... Would there be anything from Solomon's files on this woman? So many files were in there that she had no way to remember all the names. And she really didn't need to go looking for more cases, but what if Solomon had something here? Solomon had been a journalist for decades.

So, on that note, she went to the closet and pulled out the four boxes. She should label them so she could grab what she wanted. Quickly she went through the files but didn't see anything with Pollock on it. She checked *M* for Meredith just to make sure, but nothing was there either. What she needed to do was to prepare a list of just the names on the file tabs. She didn't have a ready tally of what the files were yet.

Just then the doorbell rang. Doreen straightened but couldn't see anybody through the living room window. Mugs barked like crazy at the front door, whereas Goliath had gone in the opposite direction. Doreen pushed the boxes back into the front closet and closed its door, so she could answer the front door. A young woman stood in front of her. Doreen smiled at her and said, "Yes, can I help you?"

The woman gave her a luminous smile and said in a low voice, "You already have. I'm Crystal."

It took a moment for the tumblers in Doreen's brain to connect, and then she gasped in surprise and instinctively opened her arms—she didn't know why. Still Crystal threw herself into her arms, and they hugged. They stood like that for a long moment, where Doreen felt tears well in the corners of her eyes.

The animals wove in and about them, rubbing alongside their legs, giving Crystal a welcoming greeting of their own.

When the two women finally separated, Doreen smiled at her and said, "I am so delighted to see you."

"I got back in town a couple days ago," Crystal said. "I was trying to sneak out of my place and to yours without the media. I heard they haunt your place a lot too."

"They certainly have done so in the past," Doreen said, still smiling. "But thankfully they're not here right now. Come on in."

With a pot of tea between the two of them, they sat outside on the little deck, the animals nearby. Crystal explained so much of what had happened to her in her other life. "The only person I regretted leaving a little bit," she said, "was my mom. But, at that point, I was really worried about her boyfriend. I was just old enough to understand he was big trouble, so … when he would come into my room and stand in the open doorway and stare at me when he thought I was sleeping …" She shuddered.

"Did you tell your mom?" Doreen asked.

Crystal nodded. "But she didn't want to believe anything bad about him."

"And, of course, when you went missing, he fell under suspicion pretty fast."

"Good," Crystal said. "But he's still probably on the loose."

"Maybe," Doreen said. "I'd have to look up his name to see if we can get an update on what happened to him. Last I heard, he just dropped off the radar." As soon as Doreen said that though, she winced. *Dropping off the radar* in her world these days meant that the person was dead.

"I'd be happy if he did disappear," Crystal said. "He was really creepy. I couldn't understand how my mom loved him so much."

"I think it wasn't a case of your mom loving him," Doreen said quietly, "but more how she was grateful somebody loved her."

Crystal looked at her for a long moment and then nodded. "I guess the divorce from my dad really hurt her, didn't it?"

"The divorce and Mary's presence," Doreen explained. "It's one thing to have a divorce, and it's another thing to be replaced immediately by somebody your husband's been carrying on with the whole time."

"My father was always nice to me," Crystal said, "but I didn't have any illusions that he was a good man. He and my mom fought all the time, and he brought a lot of really rough people to the house. I never felt safe there. Mary was never friendly."

"With good reason," Doreen said. Then she looked at Crystal and said, "Have you been told the whole story now?"

Crystal nodded. "My mom and I have reunited, and it's really nice to have her in my life again. She's changed too. I'm happy getting to know her now."

"I'm sure you are. That's why she came to me, you know? So all this would blow apart, and we could get you back."

"But to think she actually knew or had suspicions about what had happened and didn't do anything about it ..."

"What I think is, she *did* do something about it," Doreen said. "Think about it. Because you are eighteen now, you could come home on your own. And no longer being a child gave you more options when you arrived here than before."

"I'm going to college," Crystal said. "There's a university in town I was thinking of applying to."

"That's a great idea. This is your hometown. I know it probably doesn't seem that way, after being gone so many years, but it is definitely a place that maybe you would like to live in again."

"Maybe," Crystal said. She hesitated and pushed her chair back, then settled on saying, "I just wanted to stop in and say, *Thank you.*"

"And you're very welcome," Doreen said sincerely. "I'm so very happy you stopped by. It's hard to work on these cases and not really get to know the outcomes in some instances."

"According to my mom, you've got quite a reputation in town now."

Doreen laughed. "Maybe, but you know what they say about reputations. There's bad, and then there's worse."

Crystal laughed. "Oh, that's cute. Well, in this case, I think it's a good reputation."

"Only because you're on the good side of it," Doreen said gently. "A lot of people are going to jail over this."

Crystal winced, then said, "I'll speak up in the brothers' defense. At least, as far as my kidnapping goes, I went willingly enough."

"And for good reason," Doreen said with a nod. "But you were a child and not responsible for your actions. They were adults and could have done things differently."

"I know it seems like people do the oddest things, maybe even the right things but in the wrong ways," Crystal said. "So I was wondering about becoming a lawyer." Her tone was abrupt, as if looking for some sort of approval that it would be the right thing to do.

Doreen had a hard time with that because she had such an awful opinion of lawyers as it was. So she stood and said in a quiet tone, "If that's where your heart lies, follow it. You'd make a great lawyer, a people's advocate, or a children's advocate. I can see you doing something like that."

Crystal beamed a smile at her. "Thank you. I do have to run though. I promised to meet my mother for a visit and then for lunch." And she turned, stepped back outside, gave Doreen a small wave, and dashed away.

Chapter 11

Sunday Midmorning...

D OREEN WATCHED AS Crystal waved goodbye a second
time as she headed down the cul-de-sac to the corner.
As soon as she was out of sight, Doreen took a deep breath
and let it out slowly.

"That was a visit we didn't expect," she said to Mugs.
He woofed by her side and smiled that goofy grin of his. She
reached down and cuddled him close. Then she said, "That's
the plus side of what we do that we don't often get to see,
isn't it?"

But then again Crystal had been a missing person's case.
It wasn't like she was a dead body buried somewhere with a
toe tag and a cold case number. And that made all the
difference too. Doreen walked back into the kitchen and
brought out the Solomon files again, more determined than
ever to not forget whatever was here. She painstakingly typed
a list of all the names on the folders. She was surprised
Solomon didn't have one already prepared in here, but
maybe it was because he knew them all intimately.

She opened each folder to figure out what the case was
all about. She didn't want to read through them all, but

thankfully Solomon had placed a short summary at the first page of each file. She scanned the summary for each file, and, by the time she was done, she had a pretty decent-size Word document to give her a quick overview of each file. Then she realized that, although she said she was done, she had only done one box, and she had three more to go. Groaning, she switched out the boxes and began the next one.

When her phone rang, it was Nan. "I had a visitor this morning," Doreen said in a happy but quiet voice.

"Who?" Nan asked curiously. "You don't get too many of those, do you? At least not strangers."

"No," Doreen said. And then she explained who showed up.

Nan gasped and cried out in joy. "Oh, that's lovely," she said. "I know there'll be charges all around on her case because it impacted so many other cases as well, but it's nice Crystal came to your door. How did she look?"

"Happy," Doreen said. "Delighted to be home, I think. She was content to have been reunited with her mother and happy to have something to do with her family again. She's also applying to the local university, I think, with an eye to eventually becoming a lawyer. At least at this point."

"Yes, she's young yet," Nan said. "Give her ten years, and she could be doing something completely different."

"At least now she has a new start to her adult life," Doreen said.

"Yes, dear," Nan said. "Speaking of life—a bunch of us are going down to a little restaurant off the beach. Would you like to come?"

Doreen stared at the phone in surprise. "Oh, I don't normally get a lunch invitation with a whole group of you," she said with a frown. "Why are you going to this place?"

"It's all about gardening," Nan said. "A bunch of us are garden fanatics, but we're all kind of old and doddering, so we might not be quite your cup of tea."

Doreen chuckled. "You're hardly doddering. You're spry and have a very vibrant and sharp mind."

"I know," Nan said with a note of satisfaction. "Also a really nice little bakery is beside the restaurant."

"What kind of a restaurant?" Doreen asked, wishing she hadn't had such a hefty breakfast. "I ate a big plate of spaghetti this morning."

"Oh," Nan said. "Well, why don't we pass this time then, and you can come next time."

As soon as Nan said that, she hung up and left Doreen staring at her cell phone screen. She wondered what that was all about. Nan had revoked her invitation as soon as she realized Doreen had had spaghetti for breakfast, as if there was some rule about that. It brought back images of her ex with all his rules for her. Forcing those thoughts to the back of her mind, she went back to work again. An hour went by before she knew it. She finished the second box and then closed her laptop and stood, calling the animals.

"Come on," she said. "We need to get some physical work done."

Just when she was about to head out to the backyard with her gardening gloves, the front doorbell rang again. She frowned as Mugs once again went off barking and howling at the front door. She walked to the door and opened it to see her neighbor, Richard, glaring at her, but he held something in his hand. She looked at the odd bag and frowned.

"It was in the garden," Richard said. "On the opposite side closer to my other neighbor. But I doubt it's related."

"Thank you," Doreen said, taking the item from him.

"We don't really have any answers to give you yet though."

"I didn't think so." He shrugged and said, "Answers would be good." And then he turned and stomped away.

She watched him go before turning her attention to the bag in her hand. It looked like the contents of a purse with several pieces of ID. She shuffled into the kitchen and spilled the contents of the bag onto the kitchen table and realized they were all from the same woman. Meredith Pollock, according to the IDs.

Doreen knew Mack would have a heyday if she touched the contents though, but she wasn't sure what else she was supposed to do if she wanted to examine the pieces. And then she got a bright idea. She opened her scanner, grabbed her tweezers, and gently scanned each piece into her scanner so she had a digital copy of both the front and back sides.

Then she picked up her phone, dialed, and said, "Mack?"

"Yes, it's my name. Don't wear it out," he said, with maybe a smile, but the fatigue in his voice was evident, making his attempted humor fall flat.

"Did you find any bodies on Steve's property?"

"Good morning, Doreen. How are you?" That meant she wouldn't get any answer.

"My neighbor just came back over," she said abruptly.

"Which neighbor and why do I care?"

"The one who had the handcuffs and the diamond ring." At that, she sensed a change in the air.

"And?"

"He found a few more things. He said he found these pieces closer to his other neighbor's side. I think that was just his way of saying it could have been his neighbor standing there and throwing the stuff in Richard's garden."

"What did he find?"

Doreen walked to her laptop, opened it up, and said, "Three IDs."

"What kind of IDs?" he growled.

She typed in Mack's name on a new email, attached the scans, and sent it to him. "I just sent you scans of them," she said.

"You touched them all, of course?"

"With tweezers. But you can bet that Father Time and Mother Nature had their grubby fingers all over them," she said in exasperation. "As did my neighbor. However, they're all in a bag right now, and I used tweezers to scan them in."

There was a moment of silence as he clicked on his keyboard.

"Did you get the email?" she asked.

"It's just coming in, and you could tell me more, you know?"

"I could," she said, "but a picture's worth a thousand words."

And just like that, to be perverse at the start of his day, she hung up on him.

She moved about and cleaned the teapot and cups from Crystal's visit, then realized she hadn't had a chance to even tell Mack about Crystal. As she headed back outside to the garden yet again, she thought she heard something. Probably her phone because she'd left it on the railing, so she ignored it. She wanted to get some work done, and he'd call back later either way. She worked on the garden, another four feet toward the house. But then she heard a sound behind her.

She spun around and was surprised to see Mack with his hands on his hips, glaring at her.

She raised her hands, palms up. "Now you're pissed at

me again. Why?"

"I wonder why?" he said. "Where are the IDs?"

"On the kitchen table," she said cheerfully. "And you may want to talk to the neighbor about where it was he found all this stuff."

"Remember? I'm the police," he said. "I'm pretty sure I can figure out what to do on my own."

Doreen shrugged and said, "Okay, so you're grumpy today. I got it."

"I'm grumpy because you keep hanging up on me," he said with half a chuckle. "And I know you think it's fun to do, but there are times it's just a pain in the ass because I have to drive down here."

"Right," Doreen said. She put down her shovel and walked into her kitchen, grabbed the bag, and handed it to him.

He looked at it and nodded. "So, we're getting more and more pieces. Interesting."

"I know," she said. "And those are relatively clean."

"Meaning?"

"Meaning, we haven't had rain in days," she said with an airy wave of her hand. "But you might want to consider that potentially this stuff hasn't been there long."

Mack raised his head. "Interesting point."

"And, of course, they're laminated, so the weather, rain or snow wouldn't hurt them anyway so maybe that's a moot point."

"Correct," he said with a nod.

As he turned to leave, Doreen said, "I had an interesting visitor today too."

He turned back halfway and looked at her, waiting.

"Crystal stopped by."

The gentlest of smiles whispered across his face. "Good. I'm glad she came. She told me that she wanted to, and I told her that you would be welcoming, but she was a little hesitant."

"She has no reason to be hesitant. I was so happy to see a live person at the end of her case."

Understanding came into Mack's eyes as he studied her. "It is quite hard, isn't it?"

"It is." She nodded. "So many dead. From accidents, from suicide, from murder …" She shook her head. "In this case, I'm absolutely thrilled Crystal was alive and well. We sat outside on my minuscule deck and had tea."

"Your deck's fine for now, until you decide what you want," Mack said cheerfully. Then he turned and left.

Doreen waited a moment or two and then walked around to the side of the garage to see if Mack had gone to Richard's. Sure enough, he was talking to him, and they were out in the front. She walked up to her front steps, so she'd get a better look and yet stayed out of view, just enough to see where they had found the IDs. It did look like it was close to the other neighbors' side. That was an interesting possibility.

She contemplated who lived there, but she couldn't remember. That was one of the sad facts about being here. She had met the woman on the left corner, but that woman had attacked her, and, of course, she had her grumpy neighbor, Richard. But who else resided in her cul-de-sac, she didn't remember or never knew their names. She walked back inside, her mind full of details. Surely there was some way to get more answers here.

Chapter 12

Sunday Afternoon ...

T HERE MIGHT BE a way to get more details, but Doreen
spent the rest of the day frustrated and upset that she
couldn't find anything relevant. Not on Meredith. Not on
where the items had been disposed of because surely somebody had a security camera pointed in that direction. But, as
far as she could see from walking around the neighborhood,
nobody did, including herself. She had asked Mack too, just
in case, but he'd responded with a no. So who knew how
long that stuff had been lying there?

She also looked for a news update on any bodies found
at Steve's place, but she had no luck. So she decided to go on
a walk to the property, only to be ceremoniously told she
wasn't allowed on the land.

She glared at the policemen, most of whom knew who
she was, and said, "The least you could do is tell me if you
found anything."

They simply grinned at her and told her to ask Mack.

She sighed as she turned around and studied the gardens
as she walked past, trying to remain positive. She worked on
Millicent's garden again on Friday. Thankfully the weeds

were under control, but they were looking at doing some transplanting. That brought Penny's garden to mind. Doreen could walk past it to see if Penny had her house for sale and whether Penny was even still there—was she out on bail? How did the gardens look now?

With the animals at her heels, Doreen made her way toward Penny's and crossed over the creek, barely avoiding getting wet. The water had risen so much that she'd ended up getting soaked on Penny's side. Good thing she'd carried both Goliath and Thaddeus.

Stopping on Penny's side, she said, "This is likely the last time, guys."

Mugs barked, completely soaked and swimming like mad to get out on the steep bank. Worried, Doreen watched him until he landed on solid ground, shaking water like crazy. She screeched slightly and stepped out of the way and then started to run around so Mugs would run too. They came up to Penny's place, but all the lights were out, the garage door was closed, and there was no sign of a vehicle.

The front garden that Doreen had created looked great. The solar garden lamp was perfect too, and the plants had settled in and apparently were getting enough water from the irrigation. She gave a happy nod and carried on. She decided not to risk returning over the creek again. Especially not when Mugs obviously had a problem getting out. So she had to walk the long way.

She came up at the small bridge that crossed to her place and walked over it. As she stopped and looked at it, she frowned. "So, who put this bridge here in the past? Who maintains it? Surely it's not the original one, considering there was such high water in the past that it took out the road bridges?

Back over on her side, she was determined to do some gardening, so she could get this side of the yard done, and they could move forward with decking plans. She worked hard and then finally crashed on her small veranda with a big glass of lemonade. She hadn't had anything else to eat since the spaghetti; yet, even now, she was doing okay, and it was two o'clock.

She checked her phone, but there were no messages. That always made her suspicious. She grabbed her laptop and found a shady spot along the wall to work on more research.

She had missed a couple emails on her phone that she hadn't been notified about. One was from Mack, confirming receipt of the IDs, while another one was from the Pioneer Society, saying they'd be delighted to take a look at what she had and asking when she could show them the items from the hope chest boxes. A phone number was at the bottom of the email, so Doreen called them and asked if it was possible to bring the stuff today. They were delighted.

Not wanting to push it off to later, she walked back into the house and brought out the boxes. She then unpacked the ones with all the lingerie and decided that everything there could go in the display, alongside the love letters. She kept scans of the love letters, and then, just because she couldn't resist, she snapped photos of the clothing too and scanned in all the pictures as well.

With that repacked and those two boxes ready to go, she still had three boxes full of dishes and one full of personal items, which she went through and decided they should go on display as well, depending on what the society wanted. And then she looked at the dishes again, laid them out, stacked them up, and took pictures of them to send to Scott.

She wouldn't give them to the society until she figured out if she wanted them herself or if Scott determined them to be a big-ticket item. And she really liked the simple pattern. With Mugs at her heels, she loaded up the car with the three boxes and headed downtown. It took her a little bit to find the society, off the Richter Street area.

When she finally found the little museum, she parked in the back, walked in, introduced herself, and then said she had the boxes in her car. She brought in the first box and showed it to them. It was all nightclothes and other clothing articles. Several of the volunteer board members were present, just concluding a meeting, and came down, delighted to see the handiwork and the personal items. Margery, the spokesperson. showed Doreen one empty glass display case. "Why don't you bring in the rest of the stuff so they could see what would fit here?"

Doreen went back to the car. Mugs, on a leash, walked by her side. She made two trips and brought in both boxes. They had the first box already unpacked and had hung them up in the glass case. The nightgowns were upstaging the other clothes, all homemade with lovely details which had turned out beautifully. As for the love letters, some of them were opened and taped to the glass so people could read it. The society staff made sure they didn't block the view of anything else. Doreen felt a sense of rightness as she watched what the women were doing.

"This is perfect," Doreen said in delight.

A few personal items Margery had put on the shelves too. And still stuff remained in the boxes, but the women gave Doreen receipts for everything as she gave them the history as far as she knew it. And then, with a happy sigh, and their promise they'd have it all properly on display the next time she came back, Doreen headed home. With that one job done, she sent the photos of the dishes off to Scott and then collapsed back down again outside. She still hadn't found out anything about this Meredith person. Nor had she eaten.

Just then Nan called her. "You should have come for lunch," she said. "It was delicious."

"I still haven't eaten since breakfast," Doreen said. "I ate so much then."

"One meal a day is one way to go through life," Nan said. "Some people even think it's the healthiest thing."

"Do you know Meredith Pollocks?" Doreen asked.

Nan's voice lowered as she said, "Meredith. Meredith. Meredith …" She paused. "Pollocks, yes, but I don't think I know a Meredith."

"She was a prostitute in town," Doreen said.

"Well, it's not like I'd know her personally then, would I?" Nan said in exasperation.

"You would if she happened to have been a child you knew or a teenager you knew or if you knew the family," Doreen said. "Just because she was a prostitute doesn't make her any less of a person."

"Sure," Nan said. "As I said, I know the Pollocks but not a Meredith." And then she gasped. "Do you mean Meredith, Jenny's daughter? Who then became Manny?"

"I think so yes." Doreen said. "I don't know who Jenny is either. Who is she?"

"A friend," Nan said. "I'll have to think about it."

"Don't hang up," Doreen said with sudden intuition. Too late. Nan was gone.

With the sun beating down on the back deck, Doreen took her laptop inside and started to research Manny

Pollock. Apparently the Pollocks had been around Kelowna for a good fifty-plus years.

Which meant, Nan would know them. Or of them. That didn't mean she knew anyone in the family anymore though. The family had a hardware store that had passed down to every generation. Doreen laughed at that. In the older days everybody used to look down on those working in a trade. Yet they were the ones with steady businesses and steady money. And, of course, that was why a lot of the wealthier people looked down on them. But Kelowna was built on pioneers and farmers and orchardists—working people. It was just that kind of area here.

Doreen continued to do as much research as she could, but there wasn't any mention of a Manny Pollock either. Of the current Pollocks, at least fifteen were listed in the phone book. She could hardly just sit here and dig down, wondering who and what. But then, there was the historical society of the pioneer families. Fifty years ago probably didn't quite count because Kelowna had been settled by the Europeans starting in the mid-1800s. Of course the aboriginal tribes roamed over this area some six thousand years ago.

She went looking for a Pollocks family tree. She should really sign up for a genealogy site. She didn't know if she could access other people's family trees or if she would just pay a fee to get hers. That was of no interest. But to have access to other people's trees, well …

She did find a Pollock family tree online, and it gave her three generations. There was a Clemente and a Dorsey in the late 1800s, and they had three sons and two daughters, of which both daughters were deceased at a very young age. Doreen took a screenshot and printed it so she could look at it a little more closely.

Three men had taken the male line down, and lots of additional kids were born per the sons, but it looked like one family had been wiped out as everyone but the wife had died all in the same year. Doreen frowned at that one and wondered if it was like a car accident or something.

That left two sons and two families, of which there was a mix of males and females, but none of them had the name of Meredith. And it could have been in the next generation down, but it still didn't help her much. Then her phone rang again. Hating the interruption, she smiled when she saw who was calling. "Hey, Nan. What's up?"

"Jenny Pollock is here at Rosemoor."

Doreen straightened. "Who is Jenny Pollock?" As she looked at the tree in front of her, sure enough, Jenny was one of the son's daughters.

"Manny's mother," Nan announced. "I spoke to her this morning."

Immediately Doreen wrote that down. "Interesting. And is Manny also Meredith?"

"She was born Meredith and chose Manny later."

"Oh," Doreen said. "Why?"

"You would probably call her transgender or whatever the newfangled term is. She switched from a Meredith to a Manny."

Doreen sat back and wondered how that would have impacted her profession. Or was it because of her choices that she ended up on the streets? That placed her in an even more vulnerable sector of society. "Did Jenny say anything about her daughter—or son—now?"

"Jenny says she hasn't had any contact with her in over ten years. The first she knew she was missing was when the police came knocking," Nan said with a little bit of excitement in her voice. "Jenny would love to have answers before she dies."

"Will that be anytime soon?" Doreen's mind went to the woman she had recently gotten a confession from, who passed away on that same day.

"Well, she's got stomach cancer," Nan said, "so it's not like she'll live much longer."

"Ouch. I don't have any answers for her, so don't go telling her that I'm looking into this," Doreen warned.

"Too late," Nan said cheerfully. "If you're asking me about Manny, believe me, you're looking into it."

Doreen groaned. "I need to know more about his life, like where Manny lived, what his lifestyle was, things like that."

"I don't know if she's willing to talk about that," she said. "Jenny is very religious."

Doreen sat back and thought about what a very religious woman would think of her daughter choosing to live as a man. Talk about family strife. "And she never accepted Meredith's choice, did she?"

"No, Meredith was supposed to get married, have children, and be a normal housewife," Nan said. "Like all daughters back then."

"Did she ever marry?"

"Yes, and she did have a son," Nan said. "His parents divorced soon afterward."

"Did Meredith raise her son?"

"For the first bit. Then he chose to go to his father's family back East."

"And he's not around here anymore?"

"No, I doubt he has anything to do with Jenny or Manny," Nan said. "According to Jenny, her grandson didn't have a lot to do with Meredith when she became Manny."

"I'm sorry for Manny," Doreen said softly. "I can't imagine anything worse than to lose all your family while trying to find yourself."

"You also have to remember the timing," Nan said. "There was a lot more judgment and a lot less acceptance back when Manny decided to make these changes."

"Making him that much braver for doing so."

"Maybe," Nan said, "but nobody has heard anything about her—him—in a long time. I'll never remember to say *he* in regard to Manny."

"I think Manny would understand. You call him whatever you are comfortable with. So Jenny didn't contact the police about him being a missing person?"

"No, the police called her because several of Manny's friends had noted that she had gone missing."

"That's very sad," Doreen said. "Surely there was some communication between Jenny and Meredith, Manny?" Doreen stumbled over the son-daughter aspect and decided Manny was hardly a child anymore. If she chose this life, well *he* was an adult.

"No, the police said the friends hadn't heard anything from Manny and were asking questions. Jenny told the cops everything she could, but there wasn't much to say, and she hadn't had anything to do with Manny since Meredith became Manny."

"So, she can't help me with any details about the time he went missing, can she?"

"I doubt it," Nan said. "And, as much as she wants answers, I think she's afraid she won't like them."

"Right," Doreen said, wincing. "She already didn't like a lot about her child's life, so she may not like very much about Manny's death."

"Manny had a difficult lifestyle, one that, of course, Jenny didn't approve of. Manny did drugs. She was an alcoholic. And her friends were all in the same profession she was in," Nan said. "So, it's understandable that prostitutes end up doing drugs and drinking."

"It is, indeed. So Jenny probably doesn't want to talk to me?"

"Not really," Nan said. "I can pump her for more information though, if you like."

"How about you don't pump her?" Doreen said drily. "Maybe just ask her a few questions about who Manny hung around with, what she knew about any of Manny's friends, where he used to live, things like that."

"I'm on it," Nan said cheerfully, and she hung up.

Chapter 13

Sunday Afternoon ...

WITH MANNY CONFIRMED as Meredith, Doreen researched Jenny Pollock's life. There was a son as well as Meredith, and that was the entire family tree. She could see why the mother had always wanted the young daughter to bless her with grandchildren. That might have caused all kinds of trouble. But Meredith *had* married, and she had had a son, who was now back East, according to Nan.

Doreen wrote down the notes and then realized it would be pretty tough to find any answer because ten years had passed. And also the fact that somebody didn't just disappear. That was when she stopped. She got up and poured herself a glass of lemonade, then sat back down and opened the scans she'd made.

The IDs were all under Meredith's name. And was that because they were government-issued IDs, and she hadn't had an official sex change? How did that work? Doreen knew she wouldn't text those questions to Mack. So she opened up an email and typed out as much of an explanation as she could. And then she hit Send. When her phone rang again, she wasn't sure if it was Nan or Mack.

She answered it to hear Nan's voice at the other end. "Jenny wants answers but doesn't want to know details."

"And how do you get one without the other?" Doreen asked.

"She doesn't want anything that'll be upsetting. She doesn't have any idea who Manny's friends were, and she doesn't have any idea who her coworkers were, but she does want to know if Manny is alive or dead."

"She hasn't had anything to do with him since he took this path. Why would she care now?" Doreen asked curiously.

"Because Jenny is the keeper of the family Bible with the family tree," Nan said pointedly. "And I think she wants to make sure she has the correct entries in the Bible."

Doreen sat back with a *thunk*. "Nan, that's so cold."

"It is," Nan said. "But Jenny is not exactly a warm and welcoming woman. So, you can see how maybe Meredith, feeling like she had no support and no love anyway, might have decided to make the choices she needed to make for her own happiness."

"We can't judge her for that," Doreen said. "We all need to do what's right for ourselves."

"Exactly," Nan said cheerfully. "Which is why you let Mack teach you how to cook."

And, on that note, she hung up, but her laughter still rang through Doreen's phone long after she was gone.

Doreen placed her phone down and shrugged. Was that why she was letting Mack teach her how to cook? She really enjoyed spending time with him. He was also a great source of information, and he'd been a huge help in all areas of her life. Just his assistance in dealing with the antiques was massive alone. Was it wrong of her to build a friendship with him? She hadn't had friends—real friends—*ever* that she could remember. She'd always been guided to having the *right* friends. The ones who could take her places. Whereas right now, she liked somebody who treated her normally and was comfortable being themselves around her.

Talk about synchronicity—an email came in.

She read it out loud. "*The file mentions that he led an interesting life and was sexually attracted to both sexes. No medical records indicate a sex change had been started or completed, but, since we have no body, and we just have a missing person report, it's hard to say.*"

So, once again, not helpful. She slapped down the lid to her laptop, stood, and said, "One thing I do know is, I've spent all day without food since breakfast, and now I'm starving." And, in truth, she'd spent all day pushing the idea of spaghetti out of her mind so she didn't have a second plate too early. But she was giving up on that idea now. She planned on having a second plate as soon as she could warm it up. Only before she could get to it, the doorbell rang. She groaned. "Okay, this is just way too much company," she announced. But still, she rushed to the front door and opened it. Her neighbor Richard, complete with his grumpy face, stared at her with a glare worse than ever.

She raised an eyebrow. "Did you find more stuff?"

He shook his head and said, "No, but did you see those people?"

She looked over her yard, where he pointed, and all kinds of people stood there, taking pictures.

"No," she said. "I don't understand." She looked around and saw no media vehicles. Nothing to show they were journalists. Then she saw the huge bus parked in the cul-de-sac. "Who are they?"

"*That's* a Japanese tour bus," he said. "Now you've hit the big time. We're on their damn tour route."

Then, as soon as he said that, he huffed and crossed the front lawn to his place, where he slammed the door hard.

And the cameras flashed, catching it all.

Chapter 14

Sunday Afternoon ...

DOREEN STARED IN horror at the group of camera-toting tourists, standing in front of her property, and the huge tour bus parked as close to the front of her house as it could get. Then she stepped back and slammed the door shut, her heart pounding. She really needed to take a picture of them though. She snatched her phone, opened the door, stepped out, and took a picture of all of them. Then she retreated to her living room and sent Mack the photo.

When there was no answer right away, she frowned at her phone and sent him another text with a question mark. And again, no answer. Fuming now, she crept into the living room and looked out the window, but the bus was gone.

"Thank God for that," she whispered.

And just then, her phone rang. It was Mack.

"About time you answered me," she snapped.

At least he would have answered it if he could have, but he was spluttering with laughter too much.

How did that even work? She glared at her phone. "It's not funny!"

"Actually," he said, trying to speak through his laughter,

"it kind of is."

"That was a *tour* bus," she said in an ominous voice. "A tour bus full of camera-toting tourists, running around and taking pictures of my place!"

"Interesting," he said, but she could tell he was still trying to hold back his mirth.

"It's not funny," she snapped again. "My neighbor came over to tell me, and that's the first I knew."

"So, this could have been going on for a while?" he asked curiously.

"How am I supposed to know? If it wasn't bad enough that I had the local media around all the time, now I made it to the tour bus route."

"And I'm sure the tourists are all delighted with that," Mack said, once again desperately trying to get the words out around the laughter.

"It's not funny," Doreen growled before hanging up. Then she stormed back into the kitchen, ignoring her heated-up spaghetti, and headed right through to the garden. For the angry temper that she was in currently, she needed something much more physical to do than eating. She grabbed her gloves and shovel and attacked the last bed in the garden on that side. At this rate, she should have it done in no time. She couldn't get the picture of all those people taking photos of her house out of her mind. Why on earth would her house end up on a bus tour? Had the news finally filtered across the ocean that there had been a murder—or three—here?

She hoped not. Besides, it wasn't like this house was any different than any other house where a murder happened every day of the week. It bothered her to think that her notoriety had gotten so big.

It was also quite possible. She let her hands and body burn through her temper until she finally stopped, gasping and wiping the sweat off her forehead. She stepped back, groaning, and then realized she had finished that whole side. With enough energy still residing within her, she grabbed the edger and cut a nice crisp line all the way along the sides. Then, using the digging fork, she worked along where the back fence had once been, loosening up the dirt and pulling away the weeds.

She noted grass alongside the house, though most of it was just weeds. She frowned and wondered if she could get some thick and heavy rubber mats or something to go all along that side. It might turn into a much nicer walkway. And it wasn't for any particular purpose other than the fact that the space existed. As she stopped and turned to look back at where the deck would be, she nodded to herself.

"That grass can come to the edge here, and the stairs can come right down to the new patio," she told herself. Then she looked back alongside the house and continued talking. "Several inches of gravel and some landscape cloth or really good tarps would fix this side up too."

But, of course, it would be even harder to get back here. She'd have to do it one wheelbarrow at a time. She groaned at the idea. But it was an option, and she knew that, if she put in a big deck here, she would need to do something about the grass anyway. Plus, even if she cut it out by its roots and removed it, that would have to get hauled away. Plus she'd have to put something down to stop the grass from regrowing again. She didn't want grass coming up through the decking boards. That would look awful.

So, no matter which way she looked at it, she would have to bring in gravel. And that meant the expense of landscape cloth too. Besides the pinch financially, she realized just how much physical work would be involved.

She sighed and stepped back from her heavy rampage-fueled work, then poured herself the last of the lemonade from the fridge. She was now tired and stressed. How did that even happen? Physical work was supposed to get rid of stress. But instead, she sat here, looking at a beautiful garden, the tension coiling through her.

With the lemonade in her hand, she walked along the garden she had managed to clean up and down to the creek bed to check on the heather. And then, tossing aside her flip-flops, she stepped into the creek, noting it was higher again. But no water gushed out of the sump-pump hoses.

Cooling her feet off helped cool the rest of her off. She bent down, washed her hands, and then splashed some water on her face. Almost immediately she felt relief from the heat and the sweat. It was too bad the river wasn't clean enough and big enough to swim in because she really wanted to do that right now.

She turned to look back at her garden and the amount of work she'd accomplished. It was looking really good. Her lemonade now gone, she picked up her glass and filled it with river water. Then she gave the heather some. With the heat these days, it would need quite a bit in order to survive the transplant.

As she stood here, looking at the backyard, she wondered just how much was doable. It would be a big summer project at this rate. She could move only so many wheelbarrows of gravel at a given time.

She walked back to study the nasty section between the house and the fence. There had been gravel in there at one time, but now the weeds peeked through. She could put some stuff on the gravel to stop the weeds from growing. Things like vinegar would help, but it would take gallons. But then again, if she did that before she put down the landscape cloth, then topped it off with the gravel, that would all help.

Just the thought exhausted her. And she'd already worn out the animals. They'd crashed on the lawn earlier and slept now.

She stepped from the backyard into the front yard, peering first to make sure nobody was there to take pictures of her. A short gate separated the ugly section from the pretty lawn in the front yard. And now, of course, it needed to be mowed, which was something she hadn't ever tried to do.

But, as she looked at the height of the grass in the front yard, she knew it wasn't something she could ignore any longer. She headed to the little shed where Nan had kept all the gardening tools and found a lawnmower. The good news was, it was electric. The bad news was, despite that, it was still large and awkward.

She pushed it around the side of the house, through the little gate, plugged in the cord, and pushed the button. A horrific noise filled the air, but it sounded like the same horrific noise she'd heard before. She moved cautiously around and, after a couple moments, found it was actually an easy thing to do. She smiled in delight as she moved it back and forth, the handle easily flipping from side to side. The only thing she had to watch out for was that darn electric cord.

Life would be a lot easier if she wasn't always in peril of running over it. It took her a bit to get the hang of it and to keep it always on one side, but it only took ten minutes to mow that little piece in the front. And, with that done, she stood back and admired her grass. It was actually lovely. What she hadn't thought to do though was put the grass catcher on the side, and now the little pieces would have to be raked. Still, it was cut, and that was something.

She carefully wound the lawnmower cord and took it back to the shed. Then she saw the grass catcher. Groaning at her stupidity, she took it off the wall hook and laid it on top of the mower for next time. She glanced around the backyard and knew she needed to mow it soon. But first, she snatched a rake and grabbed her compost bin and moved it closer to the front yard. Then she raked up the bits of grass she'd cut. There was a surprising amount because the grass had grown pretty high. Using the rake and a shovel, she loaded it into the compost bin. With that done, she headed around to the back and sighed heavily. Then she brought out the lawnmower, hooked on the grass catcher, and mowed once more.

At this point she saw no sign of her animals. Smart. When there was work to be done, they'd gone into hiding.

When she was done though, it looked very nice. Still uneven but with fresh-cut grass to a certain length. It took a lot of the rough edge off her backyard garden and gave it a really nice and pristine look. Of course, the other side of the garden was still ragged and rough, and she needed to work on that next.

She looked back to the side she'd finished and smiled, feeling proud. But then looking at it reminded her to set up watering. There was no irrigation and, from the looks of it, no hoses either. She checked through the shed and found what looked like two soaker hoses. She connected them, and they almost made it down one side to the end of the garden. She hooked it up to the house and turned on the water. And then, with a bucket, she went down to the creek, filled it with water, and gently watered the end of the garden where the soaker hose didn't reach. What she needed was a third or fourth hose to wind through the shrubbery because the garden beds were deep.

At the moment, she only had them lying up against the plants. But they should twist around them all. And now that she had done this much, she thought about all the bulbs still in the shed which she could plant. They would spruce up the early spring with color. She walked back and collapsed on the small deck. Every time she came out here now, the deck irritated her.

The minute Mack had tantalized her with the idea of building a bigger deck, she couldn't let it go. As she sat here, she thought she heard somebody in Richard's backyard. She called over, "Did you know Manny Pollock?"

The voice called back, "No. Not many of us did."

"What about her mother, Jenny Pollock?"

"You mean, his mother?"

"Oh. Yeah," she said. "I do."

"Yes, she's very involved in the church."

"All that stuff we found in your garden belonged to Manny," Doreen called out. "Of course you already knew that."

Dead silence.

Chapter 15

Sunday Late Afternoon ...

THE SILENCE EXTENDED until Doreen suddenly heard something banging up against the fence. It turned out her neighbor stood on something so he could pop his head over the edge. He had a look of complete astonishment and maybe almost fear on his face. "Are you serious?"

She nodded. "That's the IDs you found. You saw the name, I'm sure. I think the handcuffs and the ring belonged to her too, but Mack's still trying to connect all of it to her disappearance."

"That's not good," Richard said. "I didn't hire him. No way would I do that. I don't use anybody like that." He shook his head so wildly that wisps of white hair flew everywhere.

Doreen smiled at him. "Finding the items doesn't mean you did. How long have you lived there?"

"About eleven years." Then he stopped, looked up at the sky, and said, "Make that twelve."

"You might have been here when all that happened, but we think somebody stole Manny's purse from an evidence box that was being cleaned out at the police station. How it ended up in your garden, I don't know. Likely kids, but I doubt we'll ever find out for sure."

Relief crossed his face, and he bobbed his head.

Doreen watched in fascination as the same wisps of hair now changed direction and flew up and down.

"Yes, yes," he said. "That must be what happened."

She felt sorry for him. "I don't think anybody really thinks you hired Manny for his services."

"They better not," he growled. He looked toward the road and said, "Are they gone?"

She nodded. "Yes, they're gone. They didn't stay much longer than you did."

"Good. It's a darn shame when I can't even go outside my own house."

"It's not your house they're photographing," she said drily. "It's mine."

"Well, if you wouldn't be such a media hound."

"I'm hardly that," Doreen cried out in outrage. "It's not my fault I managed to solve a few cold cases."

"If it isn't yours, who else's is it?" he snapped.

"Hey, I'm not seeking the publicity but some answers for these poor families," Doreen stated.

Then his gaze caught sight of her backyard, and his eyebrows shot up. "Wow, you've done a lot here."

"I'm trying," she said grudgingly. "The garden alongside your fence is done, but I haven't done the other side yet. I just managed to find a few hoses to get some water to the garden. I don't have enough though. I need to buy more."

"Nan had lots of hoses," he said.

"Maybe, but I could only find two."

"Keep looking," he advised. "I think she had enough to go all the way to the creek on both sides."

Doreen jumped to her feet. "That is exactly what I need. I was also hoping to maybe put in a bigger deck back here."

He studied the deck and said, "You should. That one's pretty rotten."

She turned to look at it suspiciously. "Is it?"

"Yeah, it is," he said. "Sooner than later you will fall through. It's not like you'll fall deep, but you can cut yourself pretty badly on the wood."

"That's not good," she said. "I just don't have any money to hire somebody."

"You don't need to hire anybody. It's not hard." And, with that, he disappeared.

She raised both hands in frustration. "Well, thanks for that," she snapped. "But it's not very helpful. I don't know how to fix this."

"You didn't know how to solve cases either," came the answer. "But you managed to create enough havoc with that. So get on your deck. I'm sure you'll cause all kinds of chaos through that process too."

She glared at Richard through the fence, but he was right. She hadn't had any training to solve these cases, but she'd figured it out. So maybe she didn't need too much help on the deck either. But first, she needed to find the rest of Nan's hoses. She went back to the little shed and searched top to bottom. A box in the back had a jug on top, and, as she opened it, several spiders crawled out. She jumped back, shaking her hands.

"Okay, we don't need that," she said. She turned to call Goliath, and he darted inside. "How do you feel about spider chasing?" she asked.

Worse than she expected, he just looked at her and lay down in the middle of the cobwebs.

She groaned. "Well, now you're not getting in the house until you get that all cleaned off first," she snapped.

Thaddeus, who'd been on the veranda railing asleep, hopped to the ground, came over, and then hopped up onto the box. His head bobbed into the box, and he came back up with a squirming black eight-legged thing in his mouth. Then he hopped down, and Goliath chased him. Thaddeus dropped the spider with a squawk and took off.

This had Goliath looking gleeful and arrogant at the same time. Arrogant in the way a cat would play with its prey. He swiped at the spider left and right, then made more swipes. When the game then looked dull and boring, he stepped on the spider. A soft *crunch* made chills go up and down Doreen's back.

But maybe it was safe to check out the box now.

She dragged the box outside and carefully, with gloved hands, upended it. It was full of hoses. There was one hose with a hand-watering wand. Also several soaker hoses were coiled up. She quickly washed off all the coiled hoses. She'd found six soaker hoses in all, so she spread out three to use on the right side and added one to the other two along the left side.

With that done and water now thoroughly soaking the garden right to the creek, she came back, looking at the other two. "Might be enough to do the front yard," she said with a frown.

Dragging the two hoses to the front, she set one to wrap around the garden. However, she soon realized it wouldn't do anything for the front lawn. But, if she set up a sprinkler somewhere in the middle, she could probably get almost everything watered. She headed back to the shed, took a look, and, sure enough, found sprinklers. With one of them attached, she set up a sprinkler in the front lawn too. Now, she had to remember when to shut everything off. She set a timer on her cell phone and let everything get a good soak. That took care of all the hoses she'd found. Good thing Nan was a gardener. She loved her plants too and wouldn't have let them die of thirst.

With that all done, Doreen put everything else back in the shed, leaving the empty cardboard box outside for the spiders to do their thing and to hopefully disappear. Then she closed up the shed. Back in the kitchen, she put on coffee while she admired her backyard. That brought her back around to Richard's comments about how everybody knew Jenny and how Jenny was really big in the church. So big in the church she hadn't wanted anything to do with her daughter. But then, not everybody was okay with their children's choices. And apparently her neighbor did understand what Manny had done for a living. She wondered if she could talk to him again. Just then her timing for the sprinklers went off.

She headed out into her backyard, shut off the water, and called out, "Are you still outside?"

"Yes," he growled.

"Do you know any of Manny's friends I could talk to? Nobody's ever found him in all this time."

"Maybe he headed back East," he said.

"Maybe, but he would have had some friends here still."

"Peter," he said. "Peter Callahan."

"And how do you know he's a friend?"

"Because his father, Jeremiah Callahan, is a friend of mine. Peter was also a heavy drug addict, ended up working the streets, and never could get out of it."

"Is Peter alive?"

"Sure," he said, "but he's probably still doing the same old thing."

"He's got to be close to what, forty by now?"

"Probably somewhere around there. Maybe closer to fifty. Maybe he's moved on to be a pimp, or maybe he's just homeless and sitting on a street corner, looking for his next fix."

"Okay. I'll see if I can find him."

There was a shocked silence on the other side of the fence, and then, all of a sudden, her neighbor's head popped over the top of the privacy fence again. "You don't mean that, do you?" he asked.

She nodded. "How else will I find out what happened to Manny?" she said reasonably.

He thought about it for a moment and said, "I'm sure Peter can tell you about a bunch of other friends."

"I want to know who she might have been with that night."

"The cops should know about it."

"Maybe," she said, "but we have to consider the fact she wasn't reported missing for a couple days. Nobody seemed to notice she wasn't around right away."

"True enough," he said. He continued to look thoughtful as he studied her lawn. "You do good work," he said grudgingly. "Maybe you can find Manny after all."

"I hope so," she said gently. "Everybody deserves justice, even somebody who had a troubled life, like Manny did."

And, with that, her neighbor disappeared on the other side once more.

But she felt better knowing Richard understood where she was coming from. She walked back inside to look up Peter Callahan and his father, Jeremiah, who'd been her neighbor's friend. After some searching, she found Jeremiah ran one of the secondhand stores downtown. He had to be already in his late sixties, if not older, but this was like a charity secondhand store. Raising money for the homeless shelter, it said on the website.

While she was always up for a road trip, she looked down to check the time, then realized it was probably closing time already, as it was already a quarter to five. But then, she might have time for a quick trip. With Mugs not too happy with her lack of attention, she put a leash on him and took him out to the car. As she opened the door, Goliath ran in. Thaddeus stood on the step and squawked, "Thaddeus is here. Thaddeus is here."

"Really, do you all have to come?" But the answer was evident as Thaddeus flew into her front seat. She lifted him up and placed him on her shoulder, then got in behind the wheel. "Goliath, you're wearing a harness."

Not giving him a chance to argue, she slipped the harness she'd been keeping in her purse over his head. She didn't clip on the leash, figuring she might get him to wear the one first. But she'd keep the leash close, in case she needed to get control of him. Just the thought made her chuckle.

In typical Goliath fashion he lay here and stared at her. The only response she got was a flick of his tail.

She opened the garage door, loving the simple opener, then headed downtown.

At the secondhand store she walked inside, holding the door open for Goliath and Mugs. Most of the time Goliath stayed close anyway. But this was a store. And one that could potentially hold a lot of breakable items. She quickly scooped him up before he ran from her.

The man by the counter looked up and said, "We're closing in a few minutes."

"Thank you." She gave him a winsome smile and said, "You're not Jeremiah Callahan, are you?"

He frowned and nodded. "That I am. Who are you?"

Doreen identified herself.

"I know you. Should've recognized you by the animals." He snorted and said, "Well, I don't know anything about no cold cases, so you don't need to be asking me nothing."

"Except that you do," she said.

He straightened, and his gaze narrowed. "Who are you talking about?"

He was gruff but straight to the point. She kind of liked that. "Manny Pollock," she said. "And I believe your son, Peter, was a good friend."

Chapter 16

Sunday Late Afternoon …

JEREMIAH'S FACE SHIFTED as myriad emotions whispered across so fast it was almost hard to identify. Doreen still caught sadness and grief, anger and frustration, and then acceptance.

"Maybe I do know of a cold case then." He sagged into the chair on the other side of the counter, his face sagging a bit too. "Is that all you came for, or did you come to buy something?" He motioned around the store. "Take a good look," he said. "I need to make a sale today."

Her heart lurched at that. "Is business that bad?"

He shrugged. "Well, it sure ain't good."

As luck would have it, she spied a couple mugs right in the front of the store. They were a matching set, nice for coffee, with a handmade pottery look to them. She picked them up and admired them. "How much for these?"

He looked over and said, "Fifty cents."

She beamed and said, "I'll take all four." Then she picked up the four and put them on the counter. But now she was hooked, and she looked around, wanting to take some time and see if she needed anything else. Not that she needed much, but still …

"What can you tell me about Manny?" she asked, her voice pitched ever-so-slightly higher so she could continue to look around. Vases and all kinds of stuff were here. She didn't think she had a vase at home. She couldn't remember. Mack had helped her go through her entire kitchen stock, weeding it out to something much more manageable. There might have been a vase, but she didn't remember and didn't want to buy one if she had one.

She wandered through until she found a lovely serving bowl that would do for one of her salads. Thaddeus chirruped at her shoulders. She picked up the bowl, studied it carefully, checked it for chips, and contemplated its size.

Thaddeus's head bobbed up and down as he looked at it beside her.

Jeremiah called out, "That one's a dollar."

And she grinned to herself, thinking what a steal that was. What a great shop. She was really getting into this. She took the glass bowl and placed it with the cups. "You didn't answer the question."

He looked at the items on the counter and said, "A big spender, aren't you?"

"I inherited a houseful of stuff," she said apologetically.

Understanding came into his gaze, and he nodded. "Forgot about that. Nan always was a bit of a collector, wasn't she?" Then he rang up the sales and said, "You could continue to look around."

"I could," she said, "but you know what? I'm not getting any answers yet."

She tried to put steel into her voice. If he wanted her to buy something, he also needed to answer her questions. Not that she wouldn't have bought things but still. He stared at her glumly and said, "Manny was always welcome in my house. When Manny was Meredith, she was also welcome in my house too. I thought for a while she and my son would get married. Maybe it's a good thing they didn't. But, then again, maybe she wouldn't have gone on to become Manny."

"I'm sure it was a very troubling time for him," Doreen said gently. "I certainly don't judge him for that."

He nodded, obviously happy with her response. "Manny was a good person. But, once Manny and Peter were hooked on drugs, you could just see complete personality changes. They would go from stupors on the couch to being raving angry and crying out with the need for the next fix."

He sighed. "And then they'd jump up and head out, looking to get their drugs. I know perfectly well how they got their money for that. I tried so hard to get Peter clean. I did send him to rehab, but I just didn't have any money to keep doing that. Because, as soon as he got out of rehab, he headed back into trouble again."

Doreen nodded. "Understood, and I get that. I mean, thankfully it's not something I've ever had to face personally. But I get that the struggle itself is something most can't fight. Do you know what happened to Manny?"

He shrugged. "I didn't hear nothing until about a week later. I hadn't seen Manny in months at that point."

"So, you didn't know anything about his life? Who he had for friends or if he got engaged or anything like that?"

At her comment about getting engaged, he laughed. "Absolutely not," he said. "That wasn't something she ever planned on doing."

"Maybe not planned on," Doreen said, "but having been married once, maybe he wanted the security of a second marriage."

131

"What security?" He looked at her in astonishment. "She ended up divorced. How does marriage ever offer security? These days, divorce happens most of the time, and that just ends up causing nothing but financial ruin for anybody involved."

"Is that what happened to her?"

He nodded. "Her husband ended up with almost everything. And the kid half time. She ended up with nothing, moved into a small apartment, and I think it was all over the gender-identity issue. If that's the politically correct term."

"I'm not sure," Doreen said, "but that works for me. And it would have been tough if he hadn't gotten anything out of the marriage. Did he have a job?"

"Manny worked as a receptionist back then," Jeremiah said. "For one of the doctor's offices. I think a cosmetic surgeon. Manny used to talk about how much money the doctors all made and how envious she was that they could take somebody who was pretty ugly and turn them into somebody pretty gorgeous." He shook his head. "But the amount of money those surgeries cost just blew her away."

"I'm sure," Doreen said. "So, he used to work as a receptionist, then got divorced. Did he keep his job after that?"

Jeremiah nodded. "For a little while. But then she started hitting the gay bars and started hitting … You know? Different groups of people who weren't very good for her. And that led her to a downward spiral." He shook his head. "She was close to Peter and a couple women she worked with. They were pretty intense, the four of them." He shrugged. "They were all in the same industry."

"Is your son still in it?"

He shook his head. "Not really. It's not like he gets much business in that line anymore. I bring him a meal every couple of days." Tiredness and fatigue were on his face now. "It really sucks."

"I'm sorry," Doreen said. "It's got to be hard when you can't help those you love. It's such a sad scenario. Where would I find him to talk to him?"

He hesitated. "It might set him off," he warned.

Goliath took that moment to stretch toward the counter with his paws clicking the top piece. Jeremiah leaned over and stared at him in astonishment.

"In what way?" Doreen asked hurriedly.

Dragging his gaze back to her, he answered, "He gets very sad about her death."

"Does he know for sure he's dead?"

"I don't think there's any way to know for sure. If Peter knew something, he'd tell the cops."

"Right," she said. "That's good to know."

"It is," he said. "He's never deliberately broken the law until it came to the drugs. And the drugs are just that. There's not a whole lot we can do about it."

She nodded and smiled. "So then, the question really is, do you mind if I go talk to him? Is there any reason not to talk to him and to see what he might know that he hasn't shared with the police because he might not have considered it important?"

"That's possible. He does hold a certain amount of distrust for the police. Everybody in the business does."

"Of course," she said. "They're getting busted on every street corner."

Jeremiah laughed at that. "True enough." Then he thought about it for a long moment before speaking. "He's usually sleeping it off at the Pandosy corner, somewhere close to the old hotel there. When I go down, I try to hook him up with a bed for a few nights at the shelter. Get him showered and cleaned up, then have him eat some food."

"I guess there isn't enough housing for the vulnerable people in our society, is there?"

"There are shelters. But they tend to fill up fast. Peter's been pretty good about going to one shelter, and they often give him a night's sleep or a bed and a shower for helping out around the place. He sweeps the place out, taking out the garbage, things like that."

Doreen brightened at that. "Good," she said. "Maybe they let him eat some leftovers too."

He laughed. "They can only help so much with the homeless because, once the word gets out, they have every-body wanting the same thing." Then he said in all seriousness, "There is a soup kitchen, so I know he gets a meal a day. But sometimes he gets there too late, when the soup is all gone. There's only so much I can do."

"Of course," she said. "Thank you." She looked at the cups and said, "Do you have anything to carry these in?"

He picked up the four mugs, wrapped them in old newsprint, and gently put them inside the glass bowl. Then he lifted the bowl and handed it to her and said, "There. Now you have something to carry them in."

Chapter 17

Sunday Late Afternoon ...

DOREEN LAUGHED. "SURE. Why not? That works."

With Mugs at her side, Goliath now walking in front of them, and Thaddeus still on her shoulder, she returned to her car. She really did want to take another look around the secondhand shop, but Jeremiah had followed her and locked up behind her. Setting her precious possessions into the back of the car, she loaded Mugs up in the front and said, "What do you think? Should we take a trip downtown and see if Peter happens to be there?"

Mugs woofed at her. Thaddeus cackled, and Goliath stared at her, bored.

She nodded. "Right, we should."

The location wasn't too far away. Likely a ten-minute drive. Not as far as Glenmore. Finally she was getting to know the Kelowna area. As soon as she found the right set of corners, she pulled into an adjacent street, parked, hopped out, and checked to see if she needed to pay, but being a weekend, it was free. Delighted, she turned to her animals and said, "Let's go for a walk."

But rather than hitting the front street, she hit the alleyways. She came across a group of three men huddled together, snoozing on the sidewalk. She studied their faces carefully, but she didn't see any resemblance to Jeremiah. She kept on until she accidentally tripped across the shelter. Studying it, she walked around to the side, and there was a single man, sitting on a bench with a cup of coffee. He looked like a possible candidate. She walked up to him and asked, "Are you Peter?"

He raised his eyebrows in surprise but appeared friendly enough.

"I was just speaking to your father," she said, taking a seat on the bench beside him.

This time he seemed more shocked than anything. Yet he still appeared approachable.

"I'm Doreen," she said, as she reached out a hand to shake his. And then she knew she'd surprised him yet again when he shuffled his coffee to his other hand and shook hers. It was a rusty move, as if not many people wanted to do that with him anymore. His hand was dirty and dry, but she made herself shake it as if it were the best gentleman's hand in a boardroom. Then she smiled at him and said, "I don't know if you've heard anything about all the cold cases that have been closing in this town."

He nodded his head slowly. "It's about time somebody looked into them." His voice was raspy, as if he had inhaled too many cigarettes in a short time.

"Indeed," she said. "Well, I'm one of the people who has been involved."

He looked down at Mugs and looked back at her, then said with a gasp, "You're the crazy lady with the animals."

She winced at that. She lifted her hair back to show him Thaddeus, who was tucked up against her neck.

The man's eyes grew rounder. And then he reached up a hand halfway but dropped it.

"Does he stay like that?" he asked.

"Yes," she said, "most of the time. He's happy to walk around on my shoulder too."

Thaddeus lifted his head, squawked at the man, and said, "Thaddeus is here. Thaddeus is here."

Peter chuckled. "Wow, he talks."

"He does talk," she said, realizing how much of an ice-breaker the animals were in this situation. "His name is Thaddeus, and this is Mugs." And then she pointed to the cat wandering around a fire hydrant not too far away. Mugs wanted to go too, but she had him on a leash. "And that's Goliath."

Peter looked at the three and then smiled. "You're the bone lady," he said with satisfaction. "The one who's been helping out with all these cold cases."

She nodded. "Yes, that's exactly who I am."

He looked at the animals curiously and asked, "What do you want with me?"

"Manny," she said gently. "I thought maybe somebody should look into Manny's disappearance."

Instead of the reaction she expected to get, his eyes filled with tears. "I'd be so grateful," he whispered, "if you could."

"I can look, but I can't guarantee I'll find any answers," she warned him.

"Of course not," he said, "but anything is something."

"What can you tell me about his last few days before he went missing?" Doreen asked as she put her phone on Record, so she'd have it for later.

"It was business as usual," Peter said. "I've racked my brain, trying to find any clue that would make a difference, but I just never do."

"So tell me, what did you tell the police?"

He shrugged. "For a couple days, we were just sitting around, doing our usual drugs and tricks and more drugs and more tricks." His voice was neutral and without inflection, as if he'd said it many times before. "And then he took a john, and I never saw him again."

"And who was the john?"

"No clue," Peter said. "I've never seen him around here. At least, I don't think so."

"So, was that common?"

He nodded. "Yeah. Sometimes they travel here for the tricks. Sometimes their friends would direct them to other locations. Or, if they're not used to hiring prostitutes, they don't want to be seen returning to the same location too often. Kelowna is a big tourist town, so you know? Anybody who's used to hiring prostitutes doesn't think anything of hiring one in a new location."

"What about the vehicle? Can you tell me about that?"

He looked at her. His gaze was a little fuzzy as he said, "It was a truck. A black truck."

"Double cab, full-size bed, did it have lots of flashy shiny chrome on it?"

"I don't remember," he said, perplexed. "The cops didn't ask me about the truck at all."

"I'm sure they asked you what vehicle it was."

"Depending on when they asked," he said, "I may or may not have told them the truth. Because I was often under the influence of drugs myself."

"Think back now," Doreen urged. "And sometimes the best way to do that is to sit back quietly and think about your friend and the last time you saw him. Did he wave at you when he got into this new john's truck? Did he give you a thumbs-up sign? Did he smile and tell you that he'd be back in ten and roll his eyes because this guy looked like he would be a penny-pincher?"

Peter laughed at that. "It's almost like you know him because he'd do things like that all the time." He thought more about it and smiled. Then he said, "He gave me the thumbs-up sign and a little finger wave, so I'd know he was pretty excited about it."

"And that would mean what? That he would be good-looking, fit, or maybe there was money in his hand?"

"All of those things," he said. "Money was important because it was our next fix."

"Did he do tricks for you to get drugs too?" she asked gently.

He nodded. "Sometimes. It's been six months since I had my last hit. It's hard, but I'm slowly weaning my way off them."

She looked at him in delight. "That's wonderful news. You should tell your father. He'd be so proud."

"I don't want to tell him," Peter said. "Not yet. Not until I make it a whole year. It seems like ten days forward and one day back, and I know how easy it is to slide. And I don't want to slide this time, so I don't want to tell him that I'm clean and then have a relapse and have him be disappointed all over again."

"I understand that," Doreen said. "Okay, so back to Manny. He hopped into this black truck. Did it have, you know, interesting wheels? Did it have chrome? Was Manny short? Did he have trouble getting up into the rig?"

"It had those checkered-pattern step-up sides," he said, "and a bed liner with the same thing."

"Interesting," Doreen said. "That's a good detail. And he used it to get in because he was how tall?"

"About five-seven," he said, "a little bit taller than average for a woman but not much."

"Great, and was she … he …" Doreen stopped at that point, not sure how to phrase it.

Peter looked at her curiously.

"I don't want to be indelicate," she said. "I'm not sure how to phrase this, but was he doing tricks as a man or as a woman?"

Peter nodded with understanding. "That was the thing about Manny. He would do both. It would depend on what the guy wanted. It was all about the money. Some days, if it wasn't going well, he'd dress up real pretty in the hopes of turning the day around."

Doreen wasn't exactly sure how that would work. She gave a head shake. "And, on that day, he was dressed as a guy?"

"Yes," Peter said, "and he hopped up, and they took off. I was sitting right here, and the truck headed on down that way." He pointed down the road on Richter Street.

"How long would he normally be for a job like that?"

"Sometimes they just pulled around the corner to the parking lot, and he'd hop out of there when they were done and would be back in twenty minutes," he said. "The fact that he drove away meant they'd be a couple hours."

"And you were just sitting here, waiting for him to come back?"

"I was just over there, not on this bench. Sitting on the side of the road," he said, as he pointed to the curbside, where a big garden was.

"Right. So you were sitting there, having a smoke and

waiting?"

He nodded.

"Anybody else come by?"

He shrugged. "That was a long time ago. Nothing was wrong in my mind, until I didn't see Manny. I fell asleep somewhere around here. The city park is just across from here, and I often go there to snooze."

"And when would you have expected to see him? During the night or in the morning?"

"Either or both," Peter said. "It would be a case of need. You know? I'd have seen him in the nighttime, if he came and woke me up or if I happened to be awake. Or at least in the morning."

"Where would he sleep?"

"In a bed with the john, if he could. Otherwise, sometimes he'd sleep on this bench or across the road in the park with me."

"So neither of you had rooms anywhere?"

"No, all our money went to drugs. As I look back, all I see is wasted lives."

"But remember. You're doing something about it now," Doreen said. "For six months. And that is something you should reward yourself for every day. You have successfully completed six months."

"Right," he said with a smile. "Now, if I can make it past all that mentally, it would be perfect."

Doreen nodded and smiled. "I get it. Is there anything else you can tell me? Did Manny have any enemies? Did anybody make any threats against him? Do you think any other women around at that time might have wanted that john for their own?"

"Those are good questions," Peter said in admiration. "I

don't think the cops asked me anything like that either."

"Well, let's ask them now, and see what we can come up with."

Chapter 18

Sunday Dinnertime ...

DOREEN SETTLED INTO a more comfortable sitting position and prepared to listen.

"He didn't get along with a lot of the other women or men. A group of transvestites hung around here, but they were more of their own group, so he didn't really fit in with them either."

"Often people who don't fit into any group form their own group," Doreen said quietly.

"That was us," he said. "Manny and I had been friends a long time before all this. I knew him as Meredith for years, so it wasn't exactly a surprise when he finally came out of the closet."

"Gender changes are much more acceptable now."

"I don't think that the women were jealous of him. I think they looked at him like he was some freak."

"Which just added to his sense of alienation."

"Exactly. And, since losing him, I have just felt so alone."

"That's because it was just the two of you in your group, and, when you lose one, you lost half. I mean, it would seem like you'd lost the better half, of course."

Peter stared at her in surprise. "You're a very surprising person. That's a very deep insight, and it's exactly how I felt. It's only now, as I look back, that my mind starts to get clearer about the drugs' influence. And I see just how dependent we were on each other too."

"When you hadn't seen him by that morning, what did you do?"

"I walked up and down the streets, asking everybody if they had seen him. But nobody had. Nobody had seen the truck. Nobody had seen the john. Nobody had seen anything," he said with a shrug. "But then I was drunk or high, so getting people to talk to me wasn't easy, and everybody I asked were street people who kept to themselves anyway."

"But, if somebody was killing other prostitutes, surely they would take note."

"But nobody else has gone missing," he said. "Just Manny."

"Interesting," Doreen said, settling back on the bench. "What about Manny's family? Did he ever talk about them?"

"He talked about his son a lot, but his son went to live with his father when Manny became public about who and what he was. Occasionally he'd get depressed over what his choices had cost him, but, on the whole, Manny was a tough cookie and didn't stay down long."

"How old was the son when he left?"

"Thirteen, maybe. He didn't like what Manny was doing."

"Right, and, of course, that's sad too."

"I don't think anybody can hurt us quite as much as family," Peter said quietly.

"Exactly," Doreen said. "But it's also family who looks

after us and loves us when we need it the most."

"Then you must have a different family than me," he said with a laugh. Then he stopped, shook his head, and said, "No, that's not fair. My father's done a lot for me, and I haven't given him credit for that. I really lucked out with him as my father. I wish I'd told him."

"I think he knows. He's talked to me about you. But, like he said to me, it's hard to know how to help."

"I know. I'm really hoping I will have something good to say to him soon."

"The sooner, the better because I think he needs to know you've at least turned a corner."

"He doesn't have much of a life, does he?"

"He works at the secondhand store. I bought four cups and a bowl from him," she said with a laugh. "It was a whole three dollars."

He grinned at her. "I got this free coffee from somebody today. That probably cost them three dollars."

"I used to be wealthy," Doreen said. "And then I used to be extremely poor. Now I realize that wealth comes in many different forms, and it's not at all about money." Then she got up, turned to smile at him, and said, "If you can think of anything else to add to this, would you call me?"

"I don't have a phone," he said.

"Okay, can you use the phone at the shelter?"

"Maybe," he said. "Do you have your number? I might come up with something."

She nodded, wrote it down on her notepad, and handed it to him. "Just remember. I'm trying to help Manny. Let's at least find out what happened to him."

"Right," he said. "Manny was a good person."

Doreen stopped at that and looked at him. "Did he help

anybody? Was he friends with somebody who he might have helped or somebody who might know anything about what happened to him?"

"I don't know. He used to go to the women's shelter a lot and give them some money. Usually when he was high as a kite, so the centers sent him away all the time when he was like that."

"So he knew somebody there maybe?" Doreen asked.

"He ended up there after he, she separated from her husband, until she could get back on her feet again. But that didn't last long. She had come out at this time. So *he* went to the shelter and then in an apartment and then started on drugs, lost his job, lost his apartment, lost his son, and ended up on the streets."

"That's such a sad ending," Doreen said.

"It is for Manny. For me, well, maybe I can change my ending."

"Which was harder to get off of, the drugs or the booze?"

"Drugs," he said. "I kicked the booze as soon as Manny went missing. But the drugs were much harder. I would go in deep to forget, then wake up. It's been a slow process. Every day I would just take a little bit less instead of shooting up. I'd make sure I spread it out over three days and then four days and then five days."

She looked at him in admiration. "That's actually quite smart. I never thought about that."

"Still, it's taken me ten years," he growled.

"And what would you have done with those ten years otherwise?" Doreen asked gently. "Look at where you are. You're six months clean. Keep sight of that as something very positive you've done and let it be something you use to keep improving your life."

Peter stared at her. "You're good for me. I can't remember the last time somebody sat and talked to me as if I were a person and not a piece of garbage on the street."

"You're not garbage," she said sadly. "The world's just very messed up." With the animals in tow, Doreen waved at him and then stopped and asked, "Have you eaten today?"

He nodded. "I had a big meal at the soup kitchen. Don't you worry. I'm okay."

She smiled and said, "Remember to call me."

After that, she walked back around the corner to her car, her pets in tow. She got into the car and drove home. Inside, she felt so sad. What a life for father and son. She pulled up to the front of her garage, used the remote to open the garage door, and drove inside. As soon as she was in, she closed the door and let out the animals.

"Okay, guys," she said, "we're home."

They raced out. As she opened the door to the house, the animals tore inside. She headed for the fridge. "It'll be spaghetti again," she called out to the empty house.

"Is that a problem?"

She shrieked and turned to see Mack, leaning against the kitchen doorway.

"Were you in my house when I came in?" she demanded.

He shook his head. "No, I've been out here on the deck, waiting for you to get home."

"Oh," she said, her hand going to her chest. "I didn't even think of that."

And then she realized he wasn't standing in the open doorway. He was talking to her through the window. The *open* window. She groaned. "I guess there's no point setting the security if I leave the windows open."

She undid the security on the door, opened it up, and let him in.

"You can make coffee," he said.

"And you could cook more pasta," she said, "because, if you want spaghetti too, that'll cut into my supply of leftover noodles."

He chuckled. "Is that all you've been eating since we had it?"

She nodded. "Pretty much."

He groaned. "You need to learn to cook a few more things.'

"I do, but I really, really, really, really love this pasta."

He shook his head, put on the teakettle, and picked up the pasta pot. Then he put it on the burner and said, "How much sauce is left? Have you been rationing yourself?"

She gave a tiny shrug and then nodded. "You know that I could eat that every day for a week." She walked over to the cupboard and pulled out a large package of noodles.

He looked at it and said, "How much do you want me to cook?"

She rubbed her hands together in glee, gave him a fat grin, and said, "All of it."

Chapter 19

Sunday Dinnertime ...

MACK LAUGHED, THEN proceeded to cook the rest of the noodles. "As meals go," he said, "that's pretty cheap."

"Exactly. The initial cost of the sauce really bothered me because I was worried what seemed like an exorbitant amount of money would be gone forever, but it's so good and stretches a long way."

"It does," he said, "but you need to learn to cook a few more dishes too."

"So what are we cooking next?"

"What about those pork chops I made you?"

"Yeah, you see? You made them, and I didn't. So I haven't tried to cook them myself."

"Right," he said. "We should work on that too then."

"Sure. I'm happy with that, but I don't have any pork."

"Spaghetti tonight again," he said. "For our next lesson, how about stir fry? Do you like stir fry?"

"Love it," she said. "And it would help to get some veggies back into my diet."

He frowned at that. "Are you only eating salads for veggies?"

She nodded. "And sandwiches."

He rolled his eyes at her. "So what's the extent of vegetables in that? Lettuce, cucumbers, tomatoes, and onions?"

"And slices of bell pepper," she said, "yes."

"Okay, stir-fried celery, cauliflower, broccoli, and maybe
some Chinese vegetables in there too. I'll pick up the
ingredients, and that's what we'll cook."

"When?"

He looked at her in surprise and said, "Friday?"

She nodded. "Do we have anything to cook it in? Don't
you need a wok?"

He looked at her in consternation. "Do you have a
wok?"

"You're the one who sorted Nan's kitchen," she said drily. "So let me ask you, do I have a wok?"

He shook his head. "No, you don't."

"I should go back to that secondhand store I was at today," she said. Then she pointed at the bowl and the four
mugs. "Those cost me three dollars," she said proudly.

He picked up the mugs and said, "Hey, these are really
nice."

She nodded "And they're not chipped."

He laughed. "I don't think anybody else is bothered by
chips except for you."

"Now I have cups I can give to company," she said.
"And they were only fifty cents each."

Chapter 20

Monday Morning ...

L AST NIGHT, DOREEN hadn't gotten a chance to pump Mack for any new information. She was upset at herself for not doing that. But she didn't want to interrupt such a lovely and friendly dinner. When he'd been called to work right afterward though, he'd taken the message and, with a cryptic look in her direction, had disappeared. He left her hoping for a tidbit of something to enlighten her, but he just shook his head and took off. He did apologize for not helping with the dishes, but she was almost used to it.

She wondered idly if he had it set up with dispatch to give him a call so he could run out on her at dishwashing time. Not that she'd done much in the way of cooking either because it was all precooked, and he'd done the noodles. But now it was morning again, and she faced so many more issues and tantalizing tidbits on various cases that she felt frustrated and curious. Finally she sat down, opened up an email, and asked Mack what case he'd gone running out of the house for the previous night.

Then she huffed when she didn't get an immediate response, deciding maybe she had just enough time with the rising river water to sneak one more walk out to Steve's to see if the police dogs and policemen were all done with the crime scene.

After breakfast, she called the animals and led them outside to the back end of the creek. She stopped when she realized just how high the creek was. She gulped but guessed that she still had enough walkway to go this way and headed out along the water, trying to stay as dry as she could. Thaddeus was obviously disturbed at the change in the water depth too as he walked back and forth on her shoulder, making an odd chuckling sound.

Meanwhile Goliath walked along higher ground as much as he could. She knew that, if the water got any higher, she'd have to pick him up and carry him. Mugs wasn't too bothered, but she was more concerned about him falling into the main part of the creek, which was now moving very quickly. She walked as far up as she could and made it just to the corner of Steve's property where the river went out around a bend, and she could hop up onto his retaining wall. Technically she was on private property at this point.

She crept around the corner and took a look, but no cops appeared to be here, just the remains of the burned-down house. Freed up to walk the property, she headed toward the visible markers. She pondered at that because a crew wasn't here. And then she checked her watch and realized it was probably still early for them. Now closer to one of the markers, she noted grave-looking disturbances in the ground, but that had been refilled. When she finished counting them, her heart sank. "Six," she whispered to her animals. "What evil doings was Steve involved in?"

Not knowing if a crew was coming back right away or if they were done here—because it looked like there had been excavations and then the graves had been refilled again to stop people from falling in—she quickly scoured the property and the house itself and then walked out to the front road rather than return along the swollen creek.

So she headed back toward home, passing the nearby house where Steven had dropped his gun and where it had been later found. Nobody was out and about. It was early, and it was a weekday, and those who had gone to work had definitely already left. Back at her house, she was grateful to see no one in the cul-de-sac taking pictures of her or her house. She walked up to the front door, let herself in, and headed back to the garden, where she swung open the kitchen door and left it ajar. She put on a pot of coffee and walked back outside to sit down and to assess her day.

The walk had done a little bit to satiate her curiosity over Steve, since she figured Mack wouldn't tell her much. Chances were, the news channels would end up reporting on whatever they found on Steve's property before Doreen even found out anything. So she could only focus on what she could focus on, and, at this point, that appeared to be Manny's disappearance. But, so far, she didn't have a lot to go on. Even if yesterday's conversation with Peter had been enlightening, it hadn't given her a lead as to where to go. Well, other than that distinctive truck the john drove. She wondered about going back and asking Peter a few more questions when her phone rang.

She looked at it, not recognizing the number. "Hello," she said.

"It's Peter," the man said hesitantly.

She smiled and said, "Good morning, Peter. How are you?"

"I'm okay. I'm at the shelter using their phone. It turns

out they're okay with me making calls as long as it's not long distance."

"Good," she said. "Did you have something more to tell me?"

"I remembered something I found in my collection of belongings," he said. "It's a letter from Manny."

"Oh, excellent," Doreen said in surprise. "Why would he have written you a letter?"

"He used to do it every once in a while, when he was planning on leaving. But his plans never worked out, so he never left. He would still leave me the letter though. I think it was his way of trying to tell me that maybe I was a good person and that I should find a way to get out of this."

"I think that's a good way to look at it," Doreen said. "Does the letter say anything interesting?"

"It says he was planning on leaving. But they all said that."

"Is this the only one that you still have?"

"Yeah," he said. "And the only reason I kept it is because he disappeared soon afterward."

"Did you show it to the police?"

He hemmed and hawed, then said, "I don't know. Back then, I might have. But I might have forgotten all about it. I had a tendency to stuff my keepsakes in the bottom of my backpack and then forget about them. I still have the same pack."

"Could I have a copy of the letter?"

"You can," he said. "I'm in the office. They said they would scan and email it for me."

"Perfect." Doreen gave him her email address, adding, "I really appreciate this. I was thinking this morning and wondering if I should come down and see if you had any other information because I'm not sure what step to take next."

"I was hoping the description of the truck would help," he said. "And I know just because it had a *Y* at the end of the license plate doesn't help much, but I was hoping it would help some."

She straightened. "You didn't mention anything about the license plate. That might help." She heard him mumble something as she waited for an explanation.

"I tend to forget things," he said. "And I don't have a great memory anymore. It's probably from the drugs. I think they've eaten too much of my brain."

"So, did you tell the police about that?"

"I think so," he said. "I don't remember much else about it though. Black with the step-up sides, that crosshatch pattern in metal, and the *Y* on the plate."

"You couldn't see the driver, right?"

"No," he said.

"Not enough to even know if it was a male or a female?"

"No. I wish I had," he admitted. "Over the years, I've wished for a lot of things, but that's one of the biggest. It's more information that would help find him."

"Okay," Doreen said. "Oh, do you know any of Manny's regular johns?"

"Not really. Like I said, some were regulars, but a lot weren't."

"What about the regulars? Was there anybody you would have known?"

He snickered. "Sure. The bank manager. He came around all the time. But other than that, not really."

Doreen's instincts prodded at her. "What bank manager was that?"

"The one who used to be at the corner down here. He was fascinated with Manny's genetic condition."

"Ah," Doreen said, "the gender identity issue?"

"Yeah, but still he was female, right? So …"

"Right. Physically he was female, but he identified as male. Would you recognize the bank manager again?"

"Probably," Peter said, "but there wouldn't be any point. He's dead."

Doreen's hope sagged. "I'm sorry to hear that. What happened?"

"Killed in a car accident, I think." Then he paused. "Maybe it was a hit-and-run? Or maybe he was driving?" He groaned. "Like I said, my memory is not the same."

"What about his name? Any idea of what his name was?"

"Norbert," he said. "Norbert Watkins."

"How often would he see Manny? Considering he was one of his regular johns."

"Once a week."

"And do you know if it was an actual …" She trailed off. She wasn't sure how to put it. "What was it? A job? Or did he just like him and want to spend time with him?"

"It was a job," he said. "Manny used to laugh at him and talk about him all the time."

"That doesn't sound very nice." Doreen stared off in the distance, wondering at the conversations likely to happen after every prostitute had a session with her john.

"Manny had his peculiarities," Peter said, "so it made sense in a way. But he always used an affectionate tone when he talked about him. I think he cared."

"It's also the lifestyle," she admitted.

"Exactly," Peter said, sounding relieved.

"What about a purse? Did Manny carry one?"

"Not really. Meredith loved them, and Manny never quite got used to not having one. He kept one stashed in the back alleyway. Not money or nothing worth much. Just old IDs and stuff. And a ring that mattered to him. Only it was a fake one, so no one stole it. The cops took the purse after he disappeared. He had a few personal items in the purse, and I gave that to the cops at the time, but honestly I was so high back then, I think the bag had been already cleaned out by other people."

"Ah." Relieved to hear that explanation, which helped tie the purse into the police station, but not the contents, which most likely were tossed randomly ending up in Richard's yard, Doreen added, "I'll try to look into that bank manager's name a little more. Anybody else?"

"No. Well, there were more johns before, but he slowly lost them."

"Why is that?"

"I think it was the drugs," Peter said. "We spent all our money to buy more drugs, didn't have anything left for food or a place to stay. Manny used to have a nice room where he could take the johns to and then his tricks ended up being just in the johns' vehicles or in back alleys. Sometimes the johns had a place."

"Right," Doreen said with a wince. "And that's the stage he was at when he hopped into the black truck, right?"

"Yes," he said.

"Okay, well, if you think of anything else …"

"Check your email," Peter said.

Doreen walked over to her laptop, opened it, waited for it to load, and then checked her email. "The scan here's perfect," she said. "Thank you."

"You'll still try, right?" he asked in an anxious tone, as if worried Doreen wouldn't continue to look for Manny. "I really want to know what happened."

"I'll do my best," she promised, "but I'm not a miracle worker. I've had some success, but I don't want you thinking it's a guarantee."

"No, that's okay. It just makes me feel not quite so alone to think somebody's still looking for him."

"And I'm sure he's watching you from wherever he is," Doreen said.

There was an awkward silence, and then Peter asked, "Do you really think he's dead?"

Chapter 21

Monday Morning...

DOREEN SAT BACK and pondered that. "I guess it's possible he did run away successfully," she said. "But you know the stats as well as I do that men and women in vulnerable parts of society don't have the greatest chance at longevity. And with a suspicious disappearance like this, of course ... Unless he's cleaned up somewhere in the last ten years, which would be great, but there's a high chance he hasn't."

"His body has yet to be found though," Peter argued. "I mean, I know in my heart of hearts that he's probably gone because he would have contacted me during these last ten years, but there's always hope."

"And that's something you might have to come to terms with," she said. "If I do find out what happened, and we do find him, it could be that he's dead, and then that hope is gone."

Peter sighed. "I know, but not knowing is worse. I keep expecting him to show up around the corner every time I look somewhere. And, even though it's been a decade, and I know the chances of him coming back and showing up like that are pretty nonexistent, I still hope. Part of me knows, if he did get out, he'd never come back. I wouldn't want to."

"It's hard to say again," Doreen said, hating that Peter was hurting over this again. "The best thing you can do is focus on you and try to get yourself to wherever you need to be."

"I know," he said. "But, at the same time, it's one of those things you never quite let go of."

"Exactly," she said. "And that's why I'm looking into it."

He rang off just then.

Doreen sat at the kitchen table and read the letter attachment he'd sent her.

"*Dear Peter,*" she read. "*I know I've said this time and time again, but this time it's for real. I've got a way to get out. I want to leave all this behind. He's a good man. He's honest and true. He's somebody I trust. I know this is for the best. I promise when I get clean and healthy, I'll come back. Always with love, Manny.*"

It even had his signature at the end. The letter was heartbreaking. Doreen downloaded it and then wrote an email to Mack and sent it to him. As she sat here, studying her garden, she wondered what it would be like to lose somebody you were so close to like that. It had to be devastating. Then she had to wonder if the letter had anything to do with it. Had the police considered one of her johns as one of their suspects?

When Mack phoned a few minutes later, he said, "I've never seen that before."

She hesitantly told him about her meeting with Peter and him finding the letter in his backpack and sending it to her.

"Wouldn't it be nice if these people would give us this

information at the time when the crime was fresh and leads were hot?" Mack complained.

"Peter's the one who contacted me this morning with the letter."

"Right," Mack said. "That still doesn't mean he didn't make this up himself."

"Why would he though?" she asked as she studied the letter on her laptop. "It looks pretty scraggly."

"Exactly. It's so hard to identify the handwriting."

"He was a drug addict," Doreen argued. "I'm sure his handwriting changed on any given day."

"Maybe. I don't know what handwriting experts would say about something like that." He sighed. Fatigue was in his voice again.

"Did you get any sleep last night?" she demanded. "That call that took you away doesn't sound like you ever went back to bed."

"I've gotten a few hours but not too many."

"Will you tell me what it's all about?"

"Nope," he said briskly. "Keep your nose out of my business."

"Can you take a look into Manny's file and see if the license plate letter *Y* was ever mentioned?"

"What *Y*?"

"That's what Peter told me. It was a big black truck with those crosshatch-pattern metal step-up sides and matching bed liner and the letter *Y* was the last letter on the license plate."

Mack wrote it down and said, "I'll have to check the file. It's not a lot to go on."

"No," Doreen said, "but given the type of truck and the license plate, surely not more than a couple hundred of them are here."

"Probably something like that. Maybe even less."

"It's something to consider. Also, what about Norbert? Norbert Watkins, the manager from the bank downtown?"

"What about him?" Mack asked in exasperation. "The name means nothing to me. So, tell me about Norbert."

"He was a regular john of Manny's, once a week without fail," she said. "And he worked around the corner. I asked if maybe they had more of a friendship than a sexual relationship, but Peter seemed to think he was a john, but Manny grew to care about him."

"Did he say why?"

"No. Thinking about it now, it was probably a way to make their jobs and daily life easier."

"We all try to laugh about everything in life," Mack said. "Sometimes it's just a nervous reaction, and sometimes it's as a way to deal with the hardship."

"Oh, Peter also said Norbert died in a car accident."

"Okay. Let me check that name," Mack said, as he typed on his laptop.

"I hate to admit it, but my first thought was that it was very convenient."

"*Convenient?*"

"Yes," Doreen said. "Convenient that he's dead."

"Are you thinking he's a suspect in Manny's disappearance?"

"Well, if he was a regular person in Manny's life, you'd think that he would have been investigated."

"I'm pretty sure Peter was investigated pretty heavily," Mack said, "because he was the closest person in Manny's life." Then Doreen heard some more clicks before Mack said, "Okay, I've got the file. It says he was killed in a hit-

and-run car accident."

"So, was he in a vehicle at the time or was he walking on the street?"

"He was crossing the road downtown on Bernard at the end of the workday but a bit late, around six o'clock. He was struck by a vehicle."

"Nobody saw anything?"

"Apparently not," he said. His voice was suspiciously bland. "You know what people are like. They don't want to say anything."

"How long ago was that?"

"Ten years ago," Mack said, and then he stopped. "Damn."

"What's *damn*?"

"Well, that's about the same time Manny went missing."

"Right. So was that death faked? Do we have any way to identify that body and make sure it was him?"

"You're saying he faked his death and took off with her?"

"I don't know what I'm saying," Doreen said, "but do we have a positive ID on the body?"

"I believe so. I have to find the autopsy reports."

She heard mumbling and clicking in the background.

"His wife identified his body, and one of his employees came upon the body soon afterward."

"So he wasn't alone after working late at night?"

"Apparently this employee had gone across the street to have dinner, and, when he came outside, he found his boss lying on the street."

"So, it definitely was Norbert who died," Doreen said with a clipped nod. "Good. We need some facts here."

"What?" Mack said in a drawl. "Is that you talking facts and not just theories? You actually want evidence?"

"Not so much evidence," she said. "*Facts*. And I wanted to know for sure Norbert was dead, and he wasn't the designer behind Manny's disappearance."

"You can't know that though, can you? Because Norbert might have had something to do with Manny's death and then was killed. Or something to do with Manny's disappearance, if you're thinking he's still alive," he said, but even his tone said it was doubtful.

"I'm not really expecting him to be alive because of his line of work. We all know what a dangerous lifestyle that is."

"Unfortunately, yes. But anyway, this Norbert guy is dead."

"Can you give me a copy of that file, so I don't have to write down all my notes?"

"No," he said, "you can do a search for it, and you'll probably get a newspaper article on it because he was a bank manager."

"Fine," she said. "Can you check on Manny's case file to see if anything there mentions Norbert and that *Y* in the license plate?"

"I will," Mack said, "but I've got a meeting in ten minutes. I've got to go." And he hung up on her.

Doreen groaned but figured he'd get back to her when he could. "Hopefully he will," she said.

She sat at her laptop and looked for articles on Norbert's death. And, sure enough, found a couple. Mostly hit-and-run news where nobody was ever caught.

"Looks like it's right up my alley," Doreen said. "This is another cold case, indeed."

Chapter 22

Monday Noon ...

DOREEN CHECKED THE date that Manny disappeared and realized she didn't have an exact date. She'd have to go back and ask Peter because she couldn't just call him. She settled on looking at the date on Manny's letter and realized it was one week before Norbert the banker's death. With that noted down in her own case file, she realized she hadn't checked to see if anything in Solomon's files were about Norbert. And she hadn't gotten as far as the *W*s in those boxes either.

Shaking her head hard, she had to get something done on the rest of Solomon's files, at least preparing that index of the file names, completing her scans of each summary sheet, just to quickly know which case files Solomon had information on. As it was, she got up and headed to the closet, pulled out the third and fourth boxes, then found one with Norbert's name on it in the final box. Excited, she pulled it out and wondered why she hadn't thought about checking the complete digital copy she had made of all the files in these four boxes when she first had received them. But she had the paper file in front of her now.

Doreen was certain Norbert's file would make a fascinating read, but she was grateful for the summary. So much easier to grasp a lot of info in a short time. According to Solomon's notes, the bank manager had been accused of stealing from the bank in the months prior to his death. It had ended up as an open issue at the time of his death. He had profusely denied any wrongdoing.

Hence, even up to the point Norbert was killed, no charges had been brought against him. He'd died soon afterward. Doreen went back and checked what day of the week it was when he died. It was a Friday. That correlated with what Mack had said. That half-explained the other coworker having dinner across the street. A lot of people went out for dinner on a Friday versus during the week. But then that was a generalization she couldn't necessarily apply here.

Potentially Norbert could have just stepped out into the road and been killed, happy to have had an end to what could have been a humiliating and painful lesson about taking what didn't belong to you.

What Doreen found interesting, however, was that the area where Norbert died was just a few blocks from the corner where Peter and Manny lived and worked much of the time. Apparently that had been their corner forever. Was Norbert heading over to talk to Manny? Was he on the way to the beach to take a walk and to clear his head? Or was he just tired after working late and stepped off the road without looking first? Maybe he was heading out for another reason too, like going out for dinner. His vehicle had been still parked around the back of the bank.

That was odd. As she continued to read through Solomon's notes, it revealed more tidbits that Solomon had gleaned about the theft from inside the bank. But then Solomon's very last line was a question that asked if Norbert Watkins was guilty or if he had been set up. *Set up?* It was right in front of her in black-and-white. What if Norbert *had* been set up? His death could have been a pretty quick end to the investigation. A very convenient end to the issue if nobody kept looking for other suspects. Maybe someone else at the bank was stealing and saw Norbert as the fall guy? For that matter, maybe he wanted the money to run off with Manny?

She frowned as she tapped the table on that thought. Then wondering further, she went back to her research and found out Norbert had a wife but no kids. He was older than his wife, according to the announcement in the newspaper. By twenty years. Her eyebrows rose. Did he have money as a bank manager? He had a decent job, but that didn't make him superwealthy. Still, he must have had some spending money if he was keeping up a weekly relationship with Manny.

And did his wife know about Manny? That would have been a hard thing to accept. At least, it would have been for Doreen. Yet, at the same time, Doreen wondered if maybe the wife was happy to have Norbert's attentions focused elsewhere. She wrote down the wife's name, which was Lynette, and how she had since been married to a Dean Porter.

Noting that name, she tracked down Dean Porter. He was an investment banker. And so back into the banking world Lynette had gone. Maybe Norbert's wages were decent, but did an investment banker make better money? He might be in a private business with his own company, but Doreen couldn't find anything to prove that. But then she caught sight of the nuptials date—only thirty days after her husband's death.

"Wow, that's cold," Doreen said as she sat back. "That's really cold."

Obviously it wasn't a happy marriage if she had grieved, had buried her husband, and had fallen in love all over again within thirty days. No way to find an address online, Doreen checked the phone book and did find them listed. They lived on Dilworth Mountain. According to some tidbits she'd heard, Dilworth Mountain was one of the hoity-toity places.

"So, you moved up in life with this marriage, didn't you?" Doreen asked Lynette's picture. "Doing the social climb. Well, it's been ten years, so I wonder how that's working out for you."

What did Doreen really know? She went over the notes in her head, as she jotted them down in order. Was killed by accident? Or was it murder? Did Norbert have anything to do with Manny's disappearance? Did his wife have anything to do with Norbert's death?

"And what are the chances," Doreen mused out loud, "that the wife had something to do with her husband's death? A month to remarry is very suspicious, indeed." Then again, maybe Norbert had committed suicide by stepping in front of a bus or whatever. His life was crashing down around him, and, for all Doreen knew, he might have been in a health crisis as well.

Once again so many unanswered questions. She sent a note off to Mack, asking if an autopsy had been done or if any underlying health conditions had been found in the banker's case. Then, knowing he wouldn't get back to her anytime soon, she stood and made herself a sandwich, even as she eyed the pasta. She would save the spaghetti for dinner.

She sat outside, sharing her sandwich with the critters and realizing she should have made half a sandwich more, just so she had enough to share. She was determined to get through the third box of Solomon's research and fully index it, like she had the others. It would take her hours, and she wasn't looking forward to it.

She looked at her garden and deemed it more appealing. But then she'd done half and needed to get the other half finished.

After eating, she sat down and worked her way steadily through Solomon's third box.

It went a lot faster than she had expected. Finally, with that third box done, she put away that box and then grabbed the fourth box. She still had several hours left this afternoon. She opened the box and started working away. By the time a knock came at her door, she had only one folder left. She groaned and straightened, rubbing her lower back. Mugs barked like crazy again. She called out, "I'm coming," but, by the time she got there, Mack had opened the door and stepped inside.

He looked at her as she straightened and stretched. "Have you been out doing heavy digging again?"

She shook her head. "No, I was trying to do an index of Solomon's files and all his summaries. He had a file on the banker."

Mack's eyebrows shot up to his hairline. "He did?"

Doreen nodded. "And, since you have a digital copy of all Solomon's files too, you can go home and read it on your own time."

He laughed. "Well, what made you think to look?"

"Because I was looking for information online, and it

was a little skimpy, so it occurred to me that maybe Solomon had something. Then, when I found it, I realized I hadn't finished doing the indexing of his boxes I had inherited."

"By indexing, you mean ..."

"I mean, typing in all the names and the basics from the summary. I've already scanned in all the summaries. I figure I'll print off the index and keep it handy, so I can easily look anything up anytime I want."

"Maybe," he said. "You've got it all digitized though, so ..."

"But it's hard to search for something in all those folders if you don't have it organized with each of the names in the front."

"So, why don't you attach the index with all the summaries?"

"I was thinking of it. I renamed all the scans, so that's something. Maybe if I have a folder system and rename the folders, I'll keep everything together and have them a little more organized."

Mack stepped out on the back deck and said, "Figured you'd be out here gardening."

"I would be," she said, "if it appealed more than doing this, but I'm one folder away from finishing, and I wanted the job done." She motioned at him as she sat down and said, "I'll just do this last one real quick."

"Coffee?" he asked, while eyeing her empty cup.

"Go put some on."

"I guess I should bring you some more," he said with a laugh.

"No need," she said. "You've been feeding me enough. I can certainly share my coffee."

"Actually I was wondering if there was leftover spaghetti," he said. "I think I'm developing a craving for it."

Doreen laughed. "I had a sandwich for lunch so I could save it for dinner. Take a look and tell me how much there is."

"We ate quite a bit of it last night," he admitted.

She kept typing away, trying to ignore his actions as he made coffee and then pulled out the pasta and the leftover sauce. When she was finally done, she saved everything and put all the physical folders back inside the fourth box and put it in the front closet. She left out the banker's file though, letting it remain on the kitchen table.

"Finally done," she said. "It seems like I had so many unfinished jobs that I never quite got anywhere."

"I know the feeling. Right now, we have so many cases where we're trying to cross the *T*s and dot the *I*s, that it's pretty impossible."

"Right. I've kept you busy."

"You think?"

"Speaking of which," Doreen said, as she returned to the kitchen, "did you find six bodies on Steve's property?"

Mack straightened, looked at her, and said, "How did you know there were six?"

"I went to the property," she admitted. "All the police tape was gone, and just the markers and these horrible slashes into the property remained."

"We did find six bodies," he said. "I'm not sure if the police are done yet though."

"Do we have any IDs on the bodies yet?"

"Not yet."

Doreen nodded. "I suppose if we go the DNA route, it can take time."

"Yes, and X-rays of the teeth can help identify each

body, which is often what we end up doing. We don't have anybody to match DNA with in most of these old cases."

"By the same token, you probably don't have too much in the way of dental records either."

"Actually we do sometimes."

"Good," she said. "We're assuming it's at least the three women who Steve paid off from the house fires?"

"You know how I feel about assumptions," he said cheerfully.

Doreen rolled her eyes at him and realized he was doing something with the noodles. She walked over to see him pouring olive oil into the leftover noodles.

She looked at it doubtfully. "Do you think there's enough?"

He nodded. "There's definitely enough."

"Good," she said, "because I'm starving. That sandwich, I had to share it times three."

Then she realized Thaddeus was on Mack's shoulder.

She stared at him. "What's this? Favoritism?"

And didn't Thaddeus lean over and rub his forehead along Mack's cheek.

She shook her head at him. "You come over here, steal my food, and steal my animals."

"Hardly," he countered. "I do have some information."

She stepped back and asked, "Does it have something to do with why you were called away last night?"

He shrugged. "Kinda."

"Does it have something to do with Steve's case?"

He shook his head. "No."

"So, what then? I didn't see anything on the news yet."

"Good," he said with a note of humor. "It means that some of our methods to keep the media out of the loop worked."

"So, what's the matter then?"

"We found a set of remains."

Chapter 23

Monday Early Evening ...

"OH," DOREEN SAID, "you mean other than the six remains on Steve's property?"

Mack nodded. "Exactly."

"So, another person?" She shook her head, sad for the loss of life yet again. "Wow. That's sad."

"It is," he said. "And that's why I was out for hours, trying to see what we could find. We had to bring in an anthropologist to take a look."

"So, they were old?"

"Well, they weren't that old, but no flesh was left on them."

"Right. They were in a condition where the decomposition happened relatively quickly."

"It was actually on one of the trails out toward Paul's Tomb," he said. "The body was only partially buried and more or less just lying there for the exposure to the elements to speed up decay."

"Animal damage?"

"Some," he said. "Lots of bug activity because, of course, Mother Nature always has an answer for cleaning up her own garbage."

"Too bad humans don't," Doreen said with spirit. "Because, well, we've got a landfill issue everywhere around the world. Particularly the oceans."

"Isn't that the truth."

"Any idea who the body is?"

He shook his head.

"Sex?" she asked.

"Female."

"Age?"

"Mature, but we don't know more than that."

She frowned at that. "You should be able to tell more than just that."

He glared at her, and she shrugged.

"Height?"

"Don't have that yet either."

"You should have some idea."

He rolled his eyes at her. "If you want the general gist, we're thinking Caucasian with dyed hair because some of the strands were sitting there as if they were heavily dyed and hadn't decomposed. Probably in her early thirties to mid-thirties, and the one thing that apparently could be told was when she had had a child."

"Right," Doreen said with a nod. "The pelvis joint." And then, she stopped, her eyes going wide as she said, "Manny!"

Mack stopped what he was doing, turned to look at her, and frowned.

"That would be good. Yet bad."

He shook his head. "It would be an answer, but you know we probably have half-a-dozen missing women just from Kelowna fitting that same description?"

She stared at him in surprise. "If that's the case, why haven't I heard of them?" she demanded.

He just went back to stirring the pasta on the stovetop.

"It would be great if it was him." And then she stopped and said, "I'm sorry. That's incredibly selfish of me."

He looked at her curiously.

She shrugged. "I was just thinking about the fact that it would be nice if he had left with that fairy-tale ending he'd put into his letter to Peter and came back triumphant and successful, having kicked the drugs out of his system, and he was now happily married and doing good works for the world."

"That's a very Pollyanna-like attitude," Mack said. "Of course we want that for everybody. But chances are, it's not likely to have happened."

Doreen nodded. "I get that. How long until we know?"

Mack shrugged. "Can't really pinpoint that. A couple days to a couple weeks."

"If it is Manny, there should be some records. And her mother is of course still alive in the old folks' home, if you're looking for DNA."

"I know. I was just thinking of that. But we don't know that it is Manny yet."

"No, but if you're looking for somebody to compare it to …"

Mack pulled out his phone and sent a text but didn't tell her what it was about. When he put the phone back in his pocket, he said, "Another five minutes and we can eat."

"Good," she said as she poured coffee. "It's just enough time to have a cup of coffee."

He shook his head. "I should have put it on afterward."

"There's no right or wrong time to put on coffee. If

there's one thing I really, really enjoy now, it's coffee when I want it."

"Couldn't you have coffee before whenever you wanted it?"

She nodded. "To a certain extent, yes. But not necessarily."

"That makes no sense."

"He didn't agree with it in the afternoon or evening. He said it causes wrinkles."

At that, Mack stopped stirring to stare at the garden and to let out a very long, slow breath. "I really do want to meet this guy just one time." His tone was conversational, but there was tension in it.

"I don't," she said. "That's a part of my life that's over. I'd be happy to never see him again."

"Speaking of which, I was talking to my brother last night."

Doreen froze this time. She walked over to stand closer, so she could see his face. "And?"

He turned to look at her. "He wants to talk to you."

She winced. "You know I really don't want to go over anything, right?"

"I think there's too much to explain on the phone. He thinks you have a really good case. He wants to take you on, but there's stuff he needs to know."

"A really good case for what? Take me on for how much?"

"He said he's willing to do it for his normal fee, but it would come out of the money you got from your husband."

"And if I don't get any money from my husband?"

Mack smirked. "Then he doesn't get paid."

She stared at him suspiciously. "That doesn't sound

right. I thought lawyers always got paid."

"The occasional few will take their money out of the spoils," he said, "but they usually only do that if they think they have a really good chance of getting you something."

She thought about it, walking to the kitchen doorway, where she leaned against the open door and stared at the waning sunshine. It did make sense he would take his money out of the money she was legally due, but she also knew her ex was pretty wily. She didn't know if Mack's brother was crafty enough to go up against him.

"I'm afraid he'll end up doing all this work for nothing," she announced.

"It's possible," Mack said as he walked over to the cupboard. He pulled out two plates. "But that's his decision."

"It also depends on how much money he's expecting to get paid for his work because, if there isn't enough left over for me to make this all worthwhile, why would I bother?"

"To make your ex pay regardless," Mack said with a laugh. "That would be the number one reason most women would do it."

She stared at him soberly for a long moment. "Not me," she said quietly. "I want to move on."

"You might want to move on," he said, "but that doesn't mean that legally he doesn't owe you."

"But how much am I likely to get out of this? You know? Your brother probably wants thirty, fifty, sixty, seventy, or maybe one hundred thousand dollars," she said. "I really have no clue."

Mack named a figure in the middle of that, and she nodded.

"So, how much will I get that'll make it worthwhile to pay him to do this? I don't want revenge to be the motivator in my life. I'd do it for justice maybe. A part of me has been hurt and devastated and wants to know I really was entitled to something after all those years. But I can't do it just because it's something a lot of women would do."

He smiled at her, leaned against the stove, and crossed his arms over his chest. "And that's just one of the reasons you are so different from a lot of women."

She shrugged. "I used to be like a lot of women. Now I'm determined to be me, uniquely, whatever it is that makes me, *me*. So I need the right reasoning for doing this."

"There's the fact you would probably never have to work again."

Her eyes widened. "How does he figure that?"

"Because you were there for so much of your husband's business-building years, so you're entitled to half."

Doreen winced. "I can tell you right now, if your brother goes after that, my life's in danger."

Mack straightened and lost the comfortable slopes in his stance. "Seriously?"

She nodded. "Yes. No way he'll let me have half. He'd kill me first."

Chapter 24

Monday Evening...

MACK STARED AT her. "Are you really thinking your husband would try to kill you?"

"Yes." Doreen nodded. "He would. Half of his estate? That's probably thirty million."

At that, Mack's own jaw dropped.

She nodded. "I told you that he's wealthy."

"So why didn't he just give you enough money to live on?"

"Because he doesn't like to share," she said. "And that includes sharing even a little bit."

Mack returned to stirring the spaghetti, but she could see his movements were no longer smooth and casual. They were jerky, with the sauce splashing up the sides.

"Hey," Doreen said. "You know what? If we don't go down this path, it's not an issue."

"You can't let fear determine what's right and wrong," he said.

"Maybe," she said.

It was obvious Mack was still upset. He served dinner and scooped the sauce over the top, carried the plates to the outside table, and sat down, but he never said a word. He just stared out at the garden.

"If you want," she said, "I'll talk to your brother."

His shoulders slightly eased as he looked down at his plate before lifting his head to study her face. "If *I* want?"

She sighed. "I should probably at least hear him out."

"You should," he said, "because you don't know what he'll do to your old lawyer."

"She deserves everything she gets," Doreen said.

"And that's a separate issue entirely," Mack said. "He's going after her on his own."

"Really?" She looked at him in delight.

"Yes, because she crossed enough legal lines that he feels he needs to bring them to the attention of the board."

"Wow," she said with a smile. "Your brother's got a lot of brimstone and fire in him."

"And he hates injustice," Mack said gently. "Remember that."

"Okay. Let's shelve that discussion for another day and enjoy our spaghetti," she said as she attacked it with vigor.

"You didn't bring a spoon?"

She gave him a shamefaced look and said, "I've been eating it without lately."

He watched, fascinated, as she wrapped the noodles around on her fork, picked it up, put in her mouth, and then sucked up the rest of the noodles.

"That's how a lot of people eat it. You know that, right?"

She nodded. "And that in itself was very freeing. I always had to have the spoon in order to make it look ladylike," she said with a laugh. "So something is very satisfying about sticking it to my ex by deliberately not using a spoon."

Mack chuckled. "Now we're back to that *you being you*

matter, whatever that quintessential you really is."

"I don't even know who she is," Doreen said sadly. "I feel like I'm just starting to find out."

"Nothing wrong with that," he said. "Enjoy the journey. And may it last forever."

She stared at him in surprise and then smiled and said, "That's one of the nicest things I've ever heard anybody say."

He shrugged. "I might not be as deep a thinker as some people, but I do have my moments."

"You can cook. That's worth a lot."

"Thank you," he said, almost humbly but with a big grin on his face.

Chapter 25

Monday Evening ...

"ALSO," MACK SAID, "have you put any more thought into your deck?"

"Lots of thoughts. I've spent a fair bit of time walking around and looking at it, and I was thinking maybe either gravel and big thick mats alongside the house to stop the weeds right up to the gate at least."

"That makes sense, and I think we should price some of the materials we'll need."

"The problem with that," Doreen said, "is that I don't really know what materials or how much materials."

"Right. I can probably help you with that."

"If we could get that much figured out, I can go in and talk to somebody, get a price quote. That would give me a place to start."

"Go to the hardware stores. Several are in town. Take in the materials list and a diagram, and they can do a cost analysis and give you a quote."

"That's what I figured."

They finished their dinner and then walked into the backyard with a tape measure and a notepad. They marked off the full measurements of the deck they had decided on.

"Now," Mack said, "take that to the hardware store and see if you can get an idea of what you need for materials. Obviously also check whether you'll have to pay for a delivery or do a lot of trips to pick it all up yourself."

"I know. I was thinking about that. I don't have any way to get heavy materials in."

"No," he said, "but, as I said, this isn't a terribly big job, but also not so small we can minimize the work going into it."

"Understood," she said with a smile.

"You might want to consider if you want to put a small deck back where we found the body. Or, if you want, make that just patio straight down this side."

She frowned. "I guess I could take the deck right across at the same height, making it wider, and then have the stairs, maybe curved stairs. Or is that too much?"

Mack shrugged his shoulders. "It's not that it's too much. We'd have to consider the total cost."

While he had that thought in mind, Mack got a call from the office and had to leave again. Doreen called her animals inside, and they all went upstairs to bed. Doreen fell asleep easily, dreaming about having a big deck and maybe a barbecue for herself.

Tuesday Morning

THE NEXT MORNING, she woke up bright and early. This time Goliath lay at her feet, Thaddeus sat on the nearby windowsill, and Mugs lay right across the pillow from her, his hot breath blowing into her now-open eyes. She laughed.

This was so much better than waking up married to her ex. Still smiling, she had a simple breakfast, since she was still partly full from the previous night.

After that, she grabbed Mugs and headed to one of the big local hardware stores. It had been open for about an hour, but it wasn't busy yet. Carrying their plan, she went over to talk to the guys in one of the contractor areas. He half smiled at her. "Can I help you?"

"Yeah, I don't know anything about this stuff, but I'm trying to figure out how much the materials would cost for a deck like this." At that, she held up the picture Mack had helped her draw on graph paper.

Interested, the clerk looked at it and, on a separate piece of paper, wrote down how many cinder blocks she needed, how many braces, how many cross pieces, and how much decking board. "You'll have to take a look at the railings too. The costs varies depending on style."

Doreen's brain swirled with the information, but, as she looked at the list, it seemed almost doable. "And how much does this cost?"

"Give me five. I'll punch it in and get you an official quote. I'll hold it for seven days."

She looked at him in delight. "Really?"

He nodded. "We can get close enough that, if you decide to go ahead with the project, then you can just bring the quote back, and we can collect the materials for you and arrange delivery, if you want."

"How much would it cost to deliver all this?"

He looked down at it and asked, "Are you in town?"

She nodded and gave him her address.

"Seventy dollars, for all of it."

She stared. "That seems reasonable."

"It's why we do it," he said. "You can't expect everybody to have a big truck and the time to do multiple loads."

She nodded. "Well, give me a quote then, and I'll mull it over."

It took a little longer than five minutes for him to calculate the quote. Finally he printed it, signed it, dated it, and handed it to her. "There you go."

And, with that, she gave him a delighted smile. She took Mugs and headed back to her car and home again. At home, she studied the quote and saw it was more than she had expected. It was $2,600, just over what she got in cash for the sale of the car parts. She scanned in the quote and emailed it to Mack.

When he called her midmorning, he said, "That's a decent price."

"How do you figure?" she asked. "It's more than we were talking about."

"But we also extended the deck alongside the house where that garden bed is," he reminded her. "And we added in steps along that front piece so you can sit on them and look at the water."

She nodded as she thought about it. "I guess we did. Do you think that's a decent quote?"

"It is," he said. "If you want though, you can go to another hardware store and get another quote. We can compare their prices afterward."

"You think they'll come in cheaper?"

"Some things will be cheaper, and some things will cost more money."

"So then, what do we do?"

"We have to figure out if you save enough by splitting up the orders and getting some things from one and some things from the other," he said cheerfully. "But keep in mind the delivery costs too, whether you can get the bigger stuff all delivered for the same seventy bucks or whether you have to pay for two deliveries. Or maybe we can even do it all in one order, and I can go pick up the rest of the stuff."

Stunned, she sat back and said, "There's more to this than I figured."

Mack laughed at that.

Chapter 26

Wednesday Morning ...

DOREEN WOKE THE next morning, groggy and feeling slightly out of it. Then again she'd spent the previous afternoon doing research until her brain couldn't handle any more and had an early night. She'd hoped to wake up clear headed. Instead, it's as if she took her deck issues along with Norbert and Manny into her dreams.

Make that nightmares.

Moving slowly, she got up, had a hot shower, and worked her way downstairs. It was a gray overcast day. Maybe she hadn't dressed warmly enough. She glanced down at her short skirt and her oversized T-shirt that hung off her shoulder. Her ex would have been horrified.

On the other hand, she didn't give a damn. She put on coffee, yawned again, and wished she had braided her hair while she was upstairs. So, while standing here, looking out the kitchen window, she ran her fingers through her hair and formed a braid to run down the side of her shoulder. She shrugged and said, "Good thing nobody's here to see me then, isn't it?"

She disarmed the security, opened the door, and let

Mugs out. She had seen no sign of Goliath. He was probably hiding from the weather. Thaddeus though was muttering to himself as he stalked back and forth on the kitchen table. She put out her hand, and he hopped on.

"Good morning, Thaddeus," she said.

He rubbed his beak gently back and forth across her cheek.

She chuckled. "That's a lovely *good morning* from you. Thank you."

With his voice in an almost hoarse whisper, he said, "Thaddeus is here. Thaddeus is here."

She stepped out on the deck, while gently stroking his feathers. Every time she saw the deck now, it just made her more determined to get a new one. Maybe that was where she should start her day. She'd get a quote from the other place. Like Mack had said, it was possible to save a few hundred dollars by splitting up the order. Of course, there was no guarantee it would work out that way, but he had suggested he could maybe do a trip too.

First though, she needed food before heading off to the hardware store. It seemed so strange to not have a million things on her to-do list. She'd already done the typewritten index file for Solomon's folders, plus the scanned summary sheets on each file, and that was all sitting on her laptop for easy access.

She hadn't slept well during the night, as she kept thinking about Manny and all the weird possibilities to his case. She understood that, from a cop's perspective, there was probably very little connection between Norbert's hit-and-run and Manny's disappearance. They were one week apart and worlds apart, as far as who the people themselves were. But the connection was there because Norbert had been one of Manny's regular clients. But was that part known when the police investigation had first been launched?

As she sat outside with her first cup of coffee, her phone rang. She groaned. "People need to leave me alone early in the morning," she announced. "I've decided I'm not a morning person." But still, the insistent ring wouldn't let her go. She snatched up her phone and saw it was Mack. She hit Talk and said, "Good morning."

"It's Manny," he said, his tone abrupt. "We matched dental records."

She straightened. "Really? Wow, that was fast," she said in satisfaction. And then she winced. "I shouldn't be so happy, should I? I guess I'm just hoping for closure for his family and friends."

"No," Mack said, "but at least there'll be some answers now."

"Some," she said. "Exactly where did you find him? You mentioned Paul's Tomb. Were the remains really in a cemetery? How could you possibly find it?"

Mack chuckled. "I guess that's true somewhat. Paul's Tomb is a popular hiking spot on Knox Mountain. Manny's body was off the normal path."

"After all this time ..." Doreen said. Then she stopped and frowned. "Cause of death?"

"That's not for public knowledge yet. You know it'll be in the news soon enough."

"Well, you must have some inkling. Can't I get consultant's status or something?" she complained good-naturedly. "I'm not spreading it around. But I do need that little tidbit of information."

"Why is that?" he asked curiously. "What can you do with it?"

"It'll help me to determine whether he was killed by a john or a friend."

"How is that possible?"

He may have worked hard to keep the derisive tone out of his voice, but she heard it anyway. She clammed up and said, "I'm not talking to you if you're mean."

He sighed again. "I'm not being mean. At the moment, I can't give you a cause of death because nobody has given us a final answer yet."

She groaned. "Which means it's probably not a bullet to the head."

"You're becoming quite the little forensic scientist, aren't you?"

"I'm not a little anything," she snapped.

"Well, that depends," he said. "Did you eat breakfast yet?"

It took her a moment to handle the switch in conversation to realize he considered her skinny and wasting away. "Not yet," she said. "I'm just sitting here having coffee. I had a rough night."

His tone turned solicitous in an instant. "I'm sorry. That's not fun."

"No," she said. "I kept thinking of Norbert and Manny."

"Honestly I haven't had a chance to go through the files yet."

"Being busy isn't an excuse."

Exasperated, he snapped, "Remember my desk has high piles of things on it."

"Sure, but this could be two cold cases solved," she said cheerfully. "You have to open Manny's back up again because you found his body."

"True," he said. "Which means I need to know every-thing you know."

She snorted. "That'll take a lifetime." And she hung up on him.

Instantly her mood was much better. She danced into the kitchen, grabbed a second cup of coffee, and called the animals. Goliath shuffled toward her slowly, as if he'd just woken. He meowed, and she bent down to scoop the big tubby into her arms and carried him and her coffee in her hands, while Thaddeus perched on her shoulder, with Mugs running around her feet all the way down to the creek. There, she sat on one of the big rocks with Goliath still in her arms and Thaddeus still on her shoulder and said, "We just need to spend a little time here. This water gives me solace like nothing else."

Content, at least for the moment, Doreen sipped her coffee as she tried to figure out what finding Manny's body would mean for the investigation. Now they should get all kinds of evidence from the body, if they were lucky. Maybe even some serious forensic evidence. Paul's Tomb though, where the heck was that? She remembered she had vaguely seen it somewhere when she was cross-referencing maps, looking at other things. Probably related to the search in Glenmore for the guys who had helped Crystal escape. At the reminder of Crystal and how her life had been turned around, she brightened yet again.

"Mack said a hiking path or something," she announced to her animals. "Now why the devil would somebody take Manny out there?" She pondered on it more and then muttered, "Of course the answer is, it's fairly out of the way. But, if it's a popular hiking spot, then a ton of people and a ton of dogs could be there any given day. So his body must have been well buried."

She muttered more as she contemplated the options. But then, all of a sudden, Mugs started barking by her side, his tail wagging like mad. But instead of jumping up and turning around to see who it was, her shoulders sagged. "You might as well get the last cup of coffee from the pot," she called out.

Ten seconds later, she heard the kitchen door bang closed.

She chuckled. Mack hadn't liked her hanging up on him again. And that was likely why he was in a foul mood. Well, that was fine. She'd woken up that way, so it was okay if somebody else was too for a while. Besides, she was in a good mood now. She waited until she heard Mugs race back to the house, barking yet again as he greeted Mack.

Thaddeus whispered in her neck, "Mack is here. Mack is here."

She reached up and gently nudged his cheek. "You're such a great watchdog," she said.

Thaddeus settled in against the crook of her neck and leaned his body weight against her. She loved it when he did that. It made her feel loved. She didn't have to wait long before she heard the heavy footsteps crunching toward her. Finally Mack stepped beside her and said, "You don't even greet your visitors anymore?"

"Depends if they come in a good mood or a bad mood," she said, looking up at him. But his countenance said he wasn't pissed. She smiled up at him. "So, if you're not angry at me, I'll say hi."

Chapter 27

Wednesday Midmorning ...

DOREEN LAUGHED AT the look on his face. It was one of disgust and yet almost acceptance.

"I guess you're getting to know me well, huh?" He sat down on another large rock nearby and studied the water's movement. "The water's definitely rising."

She nodded. "It is, indeed. But I don't think it's too dangerous yet. But then, it's getting harder to reach Steve's house."

He looked at her and laughed. "Oh, well, that's a benefit of the water rising. I never considered that you were going up through the creek though."

"I travel via the creek every time I can."

"You might want to consider getting yourself a kayak."

That stopped her cold. "Seriously?"

He shrugged and said, "Why not? You're only a few houses from the lake."

"For one, I don't know how to kayak. Although I think those boards people stand on look really graceful. I mean, that would be *them* looking graceful." She shuddered. "You know I'll be the one who's upside down in the water."

He chuckled. "But you swim, don't you?"

When she didn't answer immediately, he asked again with a narrowed gaze and in a much harder voice.

She looked at him and nodded. "I know how, but I haven't had to in a long time."

"I can understand that," he said. "But, at least, you know how to survive if you get into trouble, right?"

"Maybe," she said. "I haven't tried in a long time."

He nodded. "The lake isn't far. After the high water has dropped again, you could certainly end up with a nice calm pathway to the lake for a swim."

"Would the current be a problem?"

"Not necessarily if it's slow."

"If you say so," she said with a laugh. "I'm never really sure anymore what is hard work and what isn't. I would never have considered I could do as much gardening as I have."

"You're learning a lot about yourself. That's a good thing."

"Maybe," she said. "Being single is very different than what I thought it would be."

"Yes," he said, "but that's the point. You keep challenging yourself and doing more and more. I'm not against trying out a kayak. It's been a few years, but it's quite a unique experience."

She looked at him in delight. "Is that something we could rent?"

"We certainly could, but we could also keep our eyes open for secondhand ones."

She looked at the creek, looked at her backyard, and said, "We could just leave from here, couldn't we?"

He chuckled. "Of course, that's one of the benefits of

living on the river."

She smiled. "You know what? I think that might not be a bad idea after all."

"Now that you'll have all that newfound wealth," he said, "you can consider it."

"Ha, if there is any money," she scoffed. "Speaking of which, I planned to go to the other hardware store to get a second quote on the deck material."

"Good idea. But first, I need to ask you some questions." At that, he pulled a recorder out of his pocket and laid it on the rock. Then he turned it on, lifted an eyebrow, and said, "Now, tell me exactly what you know about this case."

She groaned. "Isn't that cheating?"

He chuckled. "No, it's called using whatever sources I can. And lately you've become a hell of a source."

She laughed and said that didn't sound too bad. In fact, it sounded darn good. "Okay, I'll start from the beginning."

And so she gave him the rundown of talking to Peter's father, Jeremiah, and then to Peter and then the research she had done on Manny and Norbert the banker. Then, when she finally worked her way down to her possible theory, she said, "And, of course, you should know—like you always tell me—those are my theories and not actual facts."

He hit the Stop button on the recorder and said, "But that's not bad. I don't know if anybody made a connection between Norbert's and Manny's deaths before."

"Norbert's death was five days later," she said. "Then his wife remarried within thirty days."

Mack's eyebrows went up again at that. "That's awfully fast."

"Considering it was a hit-and-run, and nobody was ever charged, my mind immediately goes to the wife."

He snorted. "That could be you in that position."

"I tried to save my marriage," Doreen said. "And, of course, now I have no idea why I bothered. But, in Norbert's case, I think the wife was more than happy for Norbert to disappear. Also all of Solomon's notes in there talk about the suspected theft from the bank where Norbert worked was an inside job. Or a set up."

"I looked that up and printed off a copy to go into the file," Mack said. "It's an interesting read, but no charges were ever filed. Norbert died soon afterward."

"Which is sad."

"Maybe," Mack said, "but you have to think about that now and realize it might have been not so much a hit-and-run as much as a—"

"—suicide," Doreen interrupted him.

"Exactly."

"But he had Manny in his life too," she said. "Remember that. Although he'd just gone missing so …"

He gave her a sideways look.

"I get it," she said. "Manny was of that lifestyle and obviously not somebody you would expect Norbert to want to spend more time with, but they had a relationship and a long-term one apparently. And you have to consider that anybody with a long-term relationship will have feelings one way or another. Maybe Norbert was happy to end things, or maybe Manny wanted more. But then we also have to remember that ring, and maybe Norbert gave it to him."

"What would be the reasoning behind that?"

"Maybe it wasn't an engagement ring as much as a friendship ring or a promise ring, and he was promising to get out of his marriage and to run away with Manny." Doreen studied the rising creek and thought about how she liked that idea. But, when she glanced at Mack, he studied her with amusement. She frowned at him. "What's so funny?"

"You are," he said. "Even after all you've been through, you're still a romantic."

She shrugged. "I don't know what makes somebody a romantic, but I wouldn't have said I was."

"Of course not," he said, "and that's what makes it all the more endearing."

She glared at him, not sure if she'd just been insulted. But, from the grin on his face, she thought he was probably having fun at her expense again. The trouble was, she couldn't really get too mad at him because she teased him all the time too. "So, we have to find out what the cause of Manny's death was," she said. "And seriously, there'll be a lot more people than we expected in this."

"Meaning?"

"Meaning," she said, "I suspect it'll be more than one or two or both involved."

"Convoluted as usual," he said. "Meaning, was there one murderer or two murderers?"

She raised both hands in frustration. "I think the cases are connected. But I don't know if Norbert's wife killed Manny because Manny would run away with Norbert or if somebody killed both of them."

"Or there's no connection at all," Mack said, reminding her. "Just because we like to weave stories between cases doesn't mean the stories are true."

"Exactly," she said. "And I get that, but, at the same time, there *is* a connection. I think it was stronger than we figured. I also emailed you the letter Manny left for Peter. Did you read it?"

"I did. It's also in the file. And I'll talk with Peter now." Mack stood.

Doreen jumped to her feet. "Let me come," she cried out.

He looked at her, raised his eyebrows, and said, "Why? This will be an official visit."

Her mind raced from excuse to excuse, and then she beamed a smile at him. "Because he knows me, and he doesn't trust the police. I'm sure you'd get a better reception if I went with you. And he'll be distraught when you give him the news."

Mack tapped his toe on the ground for a long moment, then looked down at the animals, and said, "I suppose you'll want to bring the animals?"

"Absolutely. Peter met them all last Sunday, when I first met with him. They are great icebreakers."

Mack rolled his eyes. "But we must leave now. I have to be back at the office soon."

"Take your truck then?" she asked, and he nodded. "Perfect. I'll be ready in two minutes."

At that, she ran back into the house, calling the animals to her. Goliath raced past her and up to the kitchen door. Meanwhile, Mugs was at her heels, while Thaddeus made a weird cackling sound on her shoulder. Inside, she grabbed her purse, set the alarm, locked the door again, and then walked with Mack around to his truck in the driveway.

The animals got thoroughly excited when they realized they were going for a ride in his truck. She opened the door for Mugs, who jumped up on the floorboard and stayed there quite happily. Goliath, on the other hand, had no intention of staying low and decided to lie on the headrest but ended up across her shoulder. So, Doreen sat down with

Mugs at her feet, Thaddeus on her shoulder, and Goliath trying to take over the headrest. It took Goliath a couple minutes until he finally lay down on her lap contentedly. Thaddeus switched sides to give himself more room.

Mack looked at them and sighed heavily. Then he started the engine and drove down the cul-de-sac. "Are you expecting the town to see you as anything other than the odd animal lady?"

"Considering Peter called me the bone lady," she said, "I don't think that's fair."

He chuckled. "I've heard you referenced as the bone lady many times."

"It's better than the other name I hear," she said in a dry tone, "which is the crazy animal lady."

Chapter 28

Wednesday Late Morning ...

M ACK PARKED DOWNTOWN in one of those metered parking areas and hopped out. Then he put some money into the machine and walked around to open the door for her. Doreen made her way out, having managed to get her new leash and harness on Goliath and one on Mugs. With Thaddeus on her shoulder, she walked across the street. Just before they got to the other side though, Goliath decided he didn't want to walk with the leash. Doreen had to admit she hadn't given him much chance to get used to it yet. Goliath lay down, like on strike, until Mack scooped him up.

"A harness and a leash for a cat? This cat? Goliath?" Mack asked. "Are you serious?"

"It seemed like a good idea," she muttered. "But you know what it's like to get a cat to do anything you want them to do. They start off with all good intentions and then head in the opposite direction."

Up ahead was no sign of Peter. Doreen walked around the corner, but he wasn't there either.

"Is this where you met him the other day?" Mack asked.

She nodded. "Right here. I sat on the bench at this end, and he sat on the bench at that end. But he did say he often went to the park to sleep." She motioned across the street, where they'd just come from, and said, "Let's go check it out."

With the traffic being almost dead, they quickly made their way across the street again. And, once Goliath saw the grass, he seemed much more amenable to walking on the leash. But Doreen knew it would only work as long as he chose to go in the same direction she went. When they finally made it into the park and the heavy trees, Mack spread out a little so they could look around.

She called out, "Peter! Are you here?"

Somewhere to the left, she heard a snuffle. She walked in that direction, and, sure enough, there was Peter, curled on the ground in front of a big tree. She frowned and said, "Now I feel like I should have brought you coffee."

He opened his eyes, stared at her, and said, "I won't say no to coffee."

"But I don't have any right now," she said with a sigh.

Peter looked at Mugs, who was sniffing him up and down. "Can I pet him?"

"Sure," she said.

He reached out to give Mugs a head scratch. Mugs's tail went crazy, and that sniffer of his went even more so. And then, Peter's eyes landed on Goliath, and they widened. "Wow," he said. "I haven't seen a cat on a leash before."

"You may never again," she said darkly as she pulled on Goliath to come join them. Goliath just gave her a look, his body going in the opposite direction.

Peter laughed. "I guess you've got a ways to go in that cat training, huh?"

"Yes," she said. "Still, it's all good. We're getting somewhere, and the more he has time with the leash, the better."

Peter didn't look at all convinced, but then neither was she. Goliath just lay here sideways, his tail flicking, until he rolled over, pulling the leash even farther and forcing her to take a step closer now as he lay on his back with his forepaws in the air, just staring up at the blue sky. "He's a very unique animal," she said.

"That he is," Peter said. "Now, what are you doing back here?"

Doreen motioned to where Mack stood.

"This is my friend Mack," she said as she motioned for him to join them.

Peter looked at him and frowned. "He looks like a cop."

"He is," Doreen said cheerfully, "but he's one of the good guys."

But Mack's presence and size did little for Peter's suspicious nature.

"He has news for you," she said gently. "So, we figured you'd like to hear it personally."

Fear filled his eyes. Peter looked up at Mack and said, "What is it? What's wrong?"

Doreen squatted in front of Peter and said, "They found Manny."

His jaw dropped, and his eyes widened. And then he realized what they meant. "Dead?" he croaked.

She nodded. "I'm so sorry."

His eyes filled with tears. "It's not fair. He never had much of a life."

"I know," Doreen said gently. "And I know it's not the news you wanted to hear. It's not the news I wanted you to hear either, but they just found him yesterday, and we didn't want you to hear about it from the media."

Peter wiped his runny eyes with his dirty sleeve. "Thank you," he muttered, his voice still choked with tears. He looked over at Mack. "When and how did he die? And will you guys care now, when you didn't back then?"

Doreen reached out a hand and gently rubbed his forearm. "They tried back then, honest. But it's hard to know what could have happened to him. Remember? You didn't have any information to help them out with either."

Shamefaced, Peter nodded. "I'm sorry. That's not fair. I was so high back then that I didn't know what was important either."

Mack crouched in front of him. "Do you have anything new to offer now?"

"Nothing more than I told her," he said, with a nod in Doreen's direction. "But maybe now that you have Manny … Maybe you can find out more?"

"Hopefully," Mack said. "That's the plan."

Chapter 29

Wednesday Noon ...

MACK DROPPED DOREEN and the animals back home an hour later. She'd done what she could to comfort Peter, though there was no comforting somebody who'd lost a friend. Not when first hearing the news. Even though Manny had been gone all these years, in his heart of hearts, Peter had hoped his friend had somehow managed to escape the lifestyle. Instead, he hadn't escaped anything. Death had come for him early.

As Doreen hopped out of Mack's truck and went to shut the passenger's side door, she looked up at Mack and said, "Let me know the details on her death, please."

With all the animals out of the way, Mack backed the truck down the driveway and headed to work. Doreen walked into the house, depressed and upset, because inside she'd hoped Manny had escaped too. As she walked into the living room and shut the door behind her, her phone rang. *Nan.* "Hey, Nan."

"What's the matter?" Nan asked sharply.

"Nothing. It's just a depressing morning."

"Oh, dear, what's wrong?"

"Nothing. I can't really talk about it right now," she said. "It's just more talking to homeless people, and you know how that lifestyle causes all kinds of hell for the families."

"You know what you need?" Nan said. "Some fresh banana muffins."

Doreen chuckled. "Nan, I think you're trying to get me fat every time you think I need something. Whether good or bad, it's always food."

"Nothing wrong with that," Nan said. "Bring the animals down here so I can cuddle them, and let's have some tea and muffins." Then she hung up on Doreen, not letting her protest.

Doreen looked down at Mugs, who was sprawled at her feet, and at Goliath, who was still on his leash, and asked, "Do you guys want to go see Nan?"

Mugs looked up at her, his ears lifting as much as his ears could lift because they sure didn't lift much. Then he woofed. On the other hand, Goliath just stared at her with his gleaming cat's eyes, while Thaddeus said, "Nan. Nan. Nan."

She looked at him and asked, "You want to go see Nan?"

"Thaddeus wants Nan. Thaddeus wants Nan," he squawked and did this real stiff-legged walk up and down her shoulder.

Doreen chuckled and said, "Okay, at least one of you said so."

She walked out the kitchen door, leaving her purse behind and resetting the alarms, then headed to the creek where she'd started her day. She left the leash and harness on Goliath, thinking it might be a perfect opportunity to get him to behave himself a little more. It wasn't that she wanted to keep him tethered, but she wanted to keep him safe. Not that they necessarily meant the same thing, but at least it was something.

She didn't rush to Nan's. Doreen was still depressed after the talk with Peter. It was good news about Manny from a closure point of view, but it was a double-edged sword of course. And seeing Peter's grief so real and so unfettered had been disturbing. At this initial point, nothing anyone could say would make him feel better. He now had to face a reality he had tried to deny for a long time.

By the time Doreen made it to Nan, she'd worked herself into a better mood. She walked across the stepping stones, watching her step. And when she hopped onto the patio and looked up, Nan gasped in astonishment as she studied Goliath.

"You've got him a harness," she said in delight. "What a great idea!"

"I don't think he thinks so," Doreen said with a chuckle.

Just then Goliath walked over to Nan, went up on his back legs, and meowed at her, as if to tell her what a hard day he'd had. Nan crouched down in front of him and gave him a really good loving.

"You're such a handsome boy," Nan said. "And you look mighty fine in that harness. The color is great for you."

Doreen raised an eyebrow. It was a brown harness on a golden cat. It was hardly a color combination that was unusual. Still, the little voice Nan was using had the intended effect, and Goliath was purring and rubbing through her arms and butting up against her chin, as if he'd not seen her for weeks and weeks.

Finally Nan had the presence of mind to realize Mugs was looking out of sorts with all the attention being poured on Goliath. Nan reached out a hand and gently scratched Mugs too. He woofed, and, even though he was lying down, he stretched out into an impossibly long version of himself just so she could reach more body parts.

Doreen sagged into a chair and said, "The animals are pathetic."

Nan chuckled. "They're honest and asking for what they want. We should all learn from that."

That was such a good point filled with wisdom that Doreen could hardly argue. By the time Nan did straighten and disappeared into the kitchen to come back with tea, all the animals were looking at her attentively. Doreen remembered how Nan usually had treats for them. Maybe that was why they wanted to come here and to see her grandmother so much.

Thaddeus walked over, tilted his head to one side, and in a proud voice said, "Thaddeus is here. Thaddeus is here."

Nan reached into her pocket and pulled out a little ziplock baggie with some sunflower seeds. She put a few down in front of him. Then she put a few dog treats in front of Mugs and a few cat treats in front of Goliath. And, with the same movement, she lifted the plate of muffins and placed it in front of Doreen.

Doreen laughed. "So am I in the same category as the pets? Is this my treat for the day?"

Nan beamed. "Why not?" she said. "I love all of you."

Doreen's heart was touched, and she whispered, "Not as much as I love you, Nan."

Nan reached across, patted the back of her hand, and said, "I'm sorry you're still having such an adjustment."

"It was a tough day," Doreen muttered. She looked at the muffins and picked up the first one. Realizing they were still warm, she took a sniff and inhaled the heady aroma of fresh banana bread. "These smell divine."

"They are divine," Nan said. "Chock-full of walnuts too."

Doreen didn't wait. She broke the muffin in half and bit in. She sat back to just enjoy it. "I don't know how you make this stuff all the time," she muttered, while looking at it. "It's all I can do to handle some basic cooking."

"It just takes practice," Nan said with an airy wave of her hand. "I've been doing this for a long time. You've got to remember that."

Doreen nodded, but she didn't think that was even one-third of the story. There was just something about the ability to walk into a kitchen and to create something magical. She polished off the first muffin and reached for the second one. As she took a bite, Nan poured her tea for her. Then Doreen realized she'd been devouring the muffins so fast it was almost rude. She forced herself to put the muffin back on the plate, settled back, and asked Nan, "How are you doing today?"

"I'm fine," Nan said, her voice almost birdlike with joy. "Had a great night's sleep last night, and it's a gorgeous morning."

Doreen looked around and shrugged. "It's overcast and gray, Nan. That's hardly a gorgeous day."

"Actually it is," Nan said. "I woke up. That makes it a good day. It's not burning hot, and it's not covered in thick smoke from fire season, so, all in all, I'll take this as a nice day."

Having made the point, Doreen could hardly argue. It was sad in a way though when Nan just waking up made it a good day for her. On the other hand, what would it take for

Doreen to have the same appreciation? "When I woke up this morning, I felt like I'd been hit by a bulldozer," Doreen said. "I had bad dreams all night of people chasing me and trying to find dead bodies, and it was awful. The coffee helped but not a lot."

"What about going downtown with Mack. Did that help too?" Nan asked in that inquisitive tone of hers.

But Doreen hadn't told Nan about that yet. "Which one of your friends tattled on me this time?" she asked with a note of humor in her voice.

Nan's smirk flashed. "It was actually the new landscaper. I was talking to him a little bit ago. He said he saw you at the city park."

"How did he know who I was?" Doreen asked in confusion. "It's not like I know who this new landscaper is."

"Oh, my dear. You went with the animals," Nan said in a chiding voice. "I don't think anybody in town now doesn't know who you are, particularly when you have them with you."

Doreen wrinkled up her face. "Okay, fair enough. Because, yes, indeed, I did have the animals with me. And, yes, I did go downtown with Mack."

"Now," Nan said, "you need to tell me why."

Doreen hesitated, not sure how much she could tell. Then she shrugged and said, "I can tell you something, but you can't pass it around. This is one of those cases that, until it hits the news, you don't get to share."

She could see the disappointment in Nan's face warring with her curiosity. Finally her shoulders sagged, and she said, "You drive a hard bargain, dear, but okay."

"It's not me driving the bargain," Doreen said. "It's Mack."

"Of course it's Mack. All those rules and regulations he has to live by," Nan said with another airy wave of her hand. "They really don't apply to people like us."

"Unfortunately they apply more to me than you might think," Doreen said with a laugh. "Not really any choice, considering I have to deal with Mack and his rules all the time."

"*You* do," Nan said smugly. "*I* don't."

Doreen rolled her eyes. "Maybe. But too often we need the cops in to deal with you as it is."

Nan just said, "Posh, don't worry about me. Now, tell me the news."

Doreen leaned forward and whispered, "They found Manny's body."

Nan gasped. "No."

Doreen nodded. "They found the body last night and identified it this morning." She found herself thinking that must be a pretty fast ID. But then she trusted Mack.

"Oh my," Nan said. "Poor Jenny."

"Why?" Doreen said in a wry tone. "So now she can make an accurate entry into her Bible?"

Nan's head shook violently. "No, no, she can't. That's the problem. And I get that times and dates don't matter to you and definitely don't matter to a lot of people, but, for something like this, accuracy is everything."

Confounded, Doreen just stared at her grandmother. "So, this is bad news?"

"Well, it's not great news obviously. We would hope Manny was alive," Nan said delicately. "But, given that she's dead, it's bad news if we don't get a date."

"A date?" Doreen asked.

"A date," Nan said with a smile. "A date of when Manny

died."

Doreen sat back and took another bite of her banana muffin. It was almost gone, but she watched her grandmother in fascination. "I can understand why a date for when Manny died is important in the investigation for finding out how she died and maybe finding out who was the killer, but surely, if we could get a general date of death, that would be enough in terms of the Bible record."

"Well, you know, anybody who records this stuff," Nan said, "they're pretty fanatical about accuracy."

"In that case," Doreen said, popping the last bite of muffin into her mouth and chewing before she said more, "Jenny might just have to wait until the police can finish their investigation."

Nan nodded slowly. "She won't like that. But I do understand, dear. You can't help it if you don't know."

"That's true," Doreen said. "And don't forget there's a good chance nobody will have an accurate date. It's not like there's ever these messages on a dead body, saying they were killed on such and such a date."

"That's inconsiderate of them," Nan said. "Surely they should understand it's important for people to know these things."

"I don't think a murderer cares," Doreen said. "A murderer is just busy trying to not leave behind little details so he doesn't get caught. He's not concerned about leaving messages behind."

"And yet some murderers do," Nan said, a knowing look on her face. "Just think about all those who tell the police where to find a body and leave them riddles and clues."

"Which is a far cry from this instance," Doreen said. "I highly doubt any note was found, saying, *I killed Manny* on such and such a date, anywhere close to the body."

"You don't have to be mocking about it, dear," Nan said. "I was just wondering."

"If and when I find out anything," Doreen said, a little ashamed of herself, "I'll tell you. But I doubt they'll even be accurate within a month or two. I guess it depends on the weather at the time."

"I don't understand any of that," Nan said, "but, if you do, that's great. I'll be happy with that, dear." Then she leaned forward and said, "Is there anything else we do know?"

Doreen shook her head. "No cause of death at this time. No time of death at this time. Basically nothing except they know it's Manny."

"Oh, that's so sad."

"Of course, and we know where Manny was found," Doreen said, staring off in the distance.

"Right," Nan said. And then, in a conspiratorial whisper, she asked, "Where?"

"Over in Knox Mountain on the way to Paul's Tomb," Doreen said. "Only that doesn't mean anything to me."

"Lots of hiking paths up that way," Nan said. "It's a big area. Lots of trails. It's popular with the locals."

"So," Doreen said, "I'm presuming Manny was in some out-of-the-way corner or otherwise hidden."

"Possibly, and we certainly haven't had any heavy rains to wash some of the dirt away that might have been covering her," Nan said thoughtfully. "So, we really have to find out how her body was discovered."

"Of course I forgot to ask Mack that," Doreen said with a sigh.

"You can ask him next time," Nan said comfortably.

And magically a third banana muffin appeared in front of Doreen. She looked at it in surprise.

"I really shouldn't have a third one," she said. But then she snatched it up and grinned. "But I really want it."

"I'm sending two more home with you," Nan said.

Doreen looked at her grandmother. "Are you keeping some for yourself?"

"Of course I am," Nan said in delight. Then she stopped and got an odd look on her face. "I wonder if Jenny knows yet?"

"No idea," Doreen said, but knowing the police would be responsible for telling her, she brought out her phone and texted Mack to see if the next of kin had been notified.

Darren was there midmorning, Mack replied.

"Richie's grandson Darren," Doreen then told Nan, "he was here this morning, talking to Jenny."

"So, whenever you're gone after tea," Nan said, "I'll go talk to her and see how she is."

"Good idea," Doreen said. "I'm sure she would like company."

"No," Nan said, "she wouldn't. But she would like somebody to commiserate about dates."

That was just too much for Doreen. She picked up the muffin and took a big bite.

Nan had a notepad out and jotted something down.

"What are you marking down?" Doreen asked suspiciously.

"I was just thinking maybe Jenny might know a little more than she's letting on."

"Such as?"

"I don't know," she said, "but surely she must know something about her daughter's life."

"It's Manny's life around the time of death that we really need to know about," Doreen said. "Who he might have been friends with, who he might have had jobs with—and, of course, I'm using the term *jobs* loosely."

Nan nodded. "It's a tough lifestyle, but I thought there was a time when the two of them communicated." She stared thoughtfully at the pad of paper, tapped her pencil on it in frustration, and then said, "I just can't remember."

"If you ask Jenny, she might remember," Doreen said comfortably.

Nan put her pencil down and said, "Very true. No point in trying to rack my brain to pull out some information that just doesn't want to be found."

When Doreen got up to leave, Nan packed up two muffins for her and handed them to her.

"Thanks," Doreen said. Then she gave the tiny woman a gentle hug and headed home.

Chapter 30

Wednesday Afternoon ...

A S SOON AS Doreen got home, she felt guilty about all the muffins she'd consumed. She changed into her gardening clothes, headed back outside with a tall glass of water and ice, and attacked the garden, starting from the creek's edge. She wasn't sure she should be working along that edge. If the water was rising, making for the rising creek, it might take away a lot of topsoil nearby. So, she started about a foot back. She was a good ten feet along when her phone rang. Ready to have any interruption to excuse her from this work, she checked the phone to see it was Nan. "Hi, Nan," she said, breathing heavily.

"With that shortness of breath," Nan said, "I would be happy if I thought you had a good reason for it. But knowing you, you're probably gardening."

Doreen groaned. "Yes, that's exactly what I'm doing. Gardening."

"Too bad," Nan said brightly. "Now heavy breathing if you were with Mack, ... that's a whole different story."

Doreen pinched the bridge of her nose and sighed. "Did you have a reason for calling?"

"Of course. It's not like I call for no reason," Nan said, puzzled.

Doreen bit back her impatience. "So what was it?"

"I talked to Jenny," she said with a note of importance. "And I knew there was something she hadn't discussed."

Doreen sank down to the grass and stretched out full length., so she could stare up at the sky as she talked to Nan. "What was it?"

"Jenny and Manny accidentally met up at City Park on one of the days Jenny was with her church group. Seeing Jenny, Manny had called to her. Jenny tried to ignore her daughter, but Manny walked over and basically embarrassed Jenny terribly in front of her church ladies."

"Of course that would be very uncomfortable for Jenny. Not exactly easy on Manny either."

"Quite right, but I think, after that, Jenny had nothing more to do with Manny."

"Did she say anything that was helpful about that meeting that would pertain to Manny's death?"

"Manny said something about how she was leaving and how Jenny wouldn't have to worry anymore."

"Interesting," Doreen said. "Did Jenny have a date when this happened?"

"Yes," Nan said, and she named the date.

Doreen thought about it and said, "That was about a week before Manny disappeared."

"Yes," Nan said. "Another reason why Jenny wasn't too worried when her daughter supposedly was missing. Because, as far as Jenny was concerned, her daughter had left, as she'd said. Jenny's pretty choked up about them finding her daughter's body now."

Doreen really wanted to ask if she was choked up about

the loss of her child or the loss of an actual accurate date of death for her family Bible, but figured that was the wrong question. "It must be tough to lose a child," she said as a compromise.

"Yes, but that's hardly Jenny's issue. I think she walked away from that whole relationship a long time ago."

"So her issue now is the date of death for the family Bible?" Doreen couldn't believe it. Surely there was something else to worry about than the accuracy of a Bible notation.

"Yes, but she also said Manny had a friend with her at the time they met. She's been trying to force her brain to think of who it was."

"And did she? Did she have a description too?"

"No, not really, but she saw Manny talking to this woman before they approached, which is one of the reasons why Jenny deliberately tried to avoid her. She was afraid it was a customer, and she didn't want anything to do with that."

"So it's this woman she's trying to identify?"

"Yes," Nan said. "And it's been bothering her."

"Right. Can she give me an age?"

"No, not really. At least I didn't think to ask."

"Nan, I'll email you a photo," Doreen said, hopping to her feet. "Can you ask Jenny if this is the woman who was talking to Manny?"

There was a short, surprised silence, and then Nan jumped in with, "Of course. You already know who it is?" Her voice rose in excitement. "Does she have something to do with Manny's disappearance?"

"I have no idea," Doreen said. "It's just a thought."

Back in the kitchen, Doreen sat down by her laptop, booted it up, and then searched for the image she was looking for. When she found it, she attached it and sent it to

Nan. "Get back to me as soon as you've asked her, will you?" Doreen asked.

"I'll call you back in ten minutes," Nan said before hanging up.

Doreen washed her face and hands while she waited to hear back from Nan. She checked the clock and realized it was midafternoon already, and she could fully justify another pot of coffee. She set one to dripping and waited. When Nan called back, Doreen snatched the phone off the table and said, "And?"

"It's her," Nan cried in excitement. "Jenny really wants to know who it is, so she has a name to go with that face."

"It's Lynette," Doreen said. "Norbert the banker's wife. That's Lynette Watkins."

"I don't know who that is," Nan said in disappointment. "I didn't recognize the face, although Jenny certainly did."

"You can tell her the name," Doreen said, "but that's not her name now. After Norbert died in the hit-and-run, she remarried fairly quickly. She married an investment banker, and her new name is Lynette Porter."

"Oh my," Nan said. "He's one of the shakers and movers in town."

"I'm not sure what that means in a small town like this," Doreen said drily. "My husband was a shaker and a mover in West Vancouver, but he was slimy."

"I'm not at all sure this guy isn't the same here," Nan said thoughtfully. "This is a fascinating turn of events."

"But really it has nothing to do with Manny's disappearance," Doreen reminded her. "All we're doing is solving the puzzle of who Jenny saw ten years ago."

"I'm telling Jenny right now." And Nan hung up on Doreen again.

Doreen chuckled. She looked down at the animals and said, "Apparently I'm a bad influence on everybody here." Mugs woofed at her, Doreen filled up his dog bowl with food, and then Goliath's and Thaddeus's. "I'm pretty sure I fed you guys, and the food is still in your bellies, but, hey, if you're hungry like I am, maybe you should have a bit more."

And rather than making herself a sandwich, she sat to have another banana muffin. And then, with the second banana muffin and a cup of coffee, she sat out on the little deck, *my very little deck*, she reminded herself. It would now only be a temporary deck though.

As soon as she finished her coffee, she would get a second quote. That would give her the information she needed. Just as she was about to finish her coffee and to head out, Nan called back again.

"Jenny says, *thank you*. That's exactly who she was thinking of. She said the woman gave Manny something. That's one of the reasons why it struck her as odd."

"Do you know what it was she gave her?"

Nan's voice rose in triumph as she said, "Yes. This woman gave Manny money."

Chapter 31

Wednesday Late Afternoon ...

THERE WERE A lot of reasons why a woman would have given Manny money. And there were many bad reasons why somebody would have done it too. But Doreen would focus on the good reasons. Maybe the woman wanted to be charitable. Maybe her husband hadn't paid last time for his *job* with Manny and had sent his wife to clear his bill. Although that boggled her mind. But it didn't mean it wasn't possible. People did all kinds of strange things.

And the truth of the matter was, that was just the way life was. Just when you thought you understood people, they went and did something strange. She couldn't jump to conclusions. Even though Jenny had identified the woman as being Norbert's wife, that wasn't necessarily enough to go on. But it was another connection between the two cases. It was also enough to go talk to Peter again. She wished he had a cell phone. She was tempted to buy him a disposable one, so, while she investigated this case, they could talk. And then her phone rang again. She stared at the unknown number. When she answered, Peter's father, Jeremiah, from the secondhand store, spoke.

In an emotional voice, he said, "Thank you."

"For what?" she asked cautiously.

"Peter's here," he said. "He's pretty shaken up, but apparently you guys found Manny."

"Yes, that's true, but it's not the end of the search. We still don't know anything about what happened to him."

"No," he said, "we know that. But we're grateful. Anything at this point is hugely helpful. I can't believe Peter's been off drugs and sober for six months." The older man's voice got tremulous.

After that, they spoke for a few more moments, and then Doreen asked, "Is it possible to speak with your son for a minute?"

"Sure, sure, sure," he said. "Hey, Peter, Doreen wants to talk to you."

In the background, she could hear Peter ask, "Who's Doreen?"

"The bone lady with all the pets, looking into Manny's case," he said in exasperation. "Come on. The woman you just talked to."

The phone was handed over, and then Peter came on the line. His voice was a little shaky as he said, "Hello?"

"Good afternoon, Peter. I hope you're feeling better."

"Not too much," he said, "but the shock's eased a bit now. That's always the worst, isn't it?"

"I think so, yes," Doreen said gently. "I did hear from Manny's mother. Of course, you know, she received the news about Manny's death today too. She did say she saw her daughter once when she was with a bunch of church ladies. Apparently she was walking in the park, and Manny came over to talk to her and ended up saying something about not having to worry about him anymore because he was leaving soon. His mom did assume at the time he had found a way to move to another part of the country. But Manny's mother also mentioned she saw somebody with him, and it took a while to figure out who it was. That woman gave Manny some money."

"Lots of people gave us money though," Peter protested. "Think about it. We were always panhandling."

"In this case though," Doreen said, "it was Lynette, Norbert's wife."

Peter gasped. "Oh, I remember that," he cried out. Then he stopped and asked, "Is it important?"

"In stuff like this," Doreen said, "it's almost impossible to know what's important and what's not. But do you know why Norbert's wife would have given Manny money?"

"A lot of reasons, I suppose," he said, "but the biggest one was she wanted Manny to disappear. She said he was a humiliation and called him all kinds of nasty names. She was a piece of work, that one. Talk about kicking somebody when they're down. That was just the person she was."

"Did she give Manny much money?"

"Yes, it was a lot," he admitted. "And I think that was why Manny was thinking she could possibly leave this time."

"Was that a condition of receiving the money? Was the wife paying off Manny, telling her to stay away from her husband or some such thing?"

"I don't think she cared about the husband one bit. I think she was hoping Manny would just disappear and would stop being an embarrassment." He sniggered. "Norbert used to talk to Manny all the time. He was really unhappily married and didn't know why he married his wife in the first place. Plus, as soon as they were married, she stopped being a wife in many ways."

"So, maybe Norbert came to Manny as much for friend-ship as anything."

"I think so, yes, and maybe more," he said. "He really was sweet on him. The weekly appointment could have been a way for him to help out Manny as well."

"True," Doreen said. "I'm glad Manny had Norbert and you as friends right up to the end."

That was the wrong thing to say because Peter started blubbering again.

"You don't happen to remember how much money it was, do you?" Doreen asked, trying to pull Peter out of it. "Or if it happened more than once?"

"It was just once," he said. "We talked about it lots af-terward because Manny was enthralled with the amount of money she'd been given. It was thousands of dollars. And it wasn't long before Manny was broke again. But he'd given everybody he knew a shot of drugs to save them from having to do at least a couple tricks."

"Sounds like Manny's actions came from heart," Doreen said with a smile. "Too bad he couldn't take that money and run with it though."

"I think he was planning on it. But he did tell Norbert, you know?"

Doreen's eyebrows shot up. "Manny told Norbert what his wife had done?"

"Yes," Peter said. "Norbert was really angry about it. When he left Manny, he told him that he'd fix it. But he did tell Manny to keep the money. He also gave him a lovely ring. Manny hawked it and bought a cheap replacement at the pawnshop. He wouldn't wear it, but Manny couldn't quite let it go. He'd been really touched."

"Well, that's good," Doreen said. She figured Manny

had probably spent all the money from Lynette and from selling Norbert's ring by the time Manny had hooked up with Norbert a week later too. "I just wonder if maybe the wife made arrangements to help Manny get out of town."

"If she did, she didn't tell Manny about it," Peter said. "Honestly, it would have been much better if she had made arrangements like that. You can't give money to a junkie. It just disappears up the arm, like everything else."

"Still, it was something. Did Manny see her again? When he didn't leave town right away, did Norbert's wife come back and yell at Manny for not having followed through?"

"I saw her myself once," Peter said. "And she didn't seem happy to see us there, but she didn't have a screaming fit or anything. I think Manny just gave her the finger as she drove by."

"Which would have pissed her right off."

"Oh, yes, absolutely," Peter said with a chuckle. "But you know what? You always get those highbrow people who think everybody else is beneath them."

Doreen knew all too well because she'd had to hang out with the highbrow people. Unfortunately she was afraid that, in the past, she may have come across as one of those highbrow people too. "If you think of any other confrontations or anybody else who might have done something odd, like that matter with Lynette, you'll let me know, won't you?"

"Nothing comes to mind," Peter said. "That was just such an odd thing. I even forgot about it until you brought it up."

"Considering it all happened fairly close in time to when Manny went missing and when Norbert died ..."

"Do you think Lynette had anything to do with Manny's death?" Peter asked, his voice suddenly dark.

"Oh, I doubt it," Doreen said hurriedly. "And remember. We can't assume anything. We need hard evidence." When she heard Mack's words rolling off the tip of her tongue, she rolled her eyes. Then she said, "Don't think or do anything rash."

"I'm too tired to do anything rash."

"I'm glad you went home to see your father," she said.

"Yeah," Peter said gruffly. "Me too."

Doreen hung up and sat here, pondering the information for a few moments. She had her suspicions, but that was all they were. Suspicions. It was too easy to get the wrong person at this stage. She sent Mack an email, telling him about the money from Lynette and the wife telling Manny to get out of town. It wasn't anything but another puzzle piece. It helped, but it didn't do a lot when the rest of the puzzle pieces were still missing. All in all, she didn't have any information that made a difference. And that was very distressing. She started in on searching for the license plate. What were the chances of finding one that ended with a *Y*? There had to be another way to do this.

Frustrated twenty minutes later, Doreen picked up the phone and dialed Mack.

When he answered, she asked, "Did you search for that truck?"

His voice was mild when he said, "Good afternoon, Doreen. You know it's almost dinnertime, right?"

She gasped and said, "Really?"

"Really," he said. "So, no, I haven't had a chance to check out that license plate. Why?"

"Because I'm wondering if anybody had that number

before."

"Remember? It's not a number. It's a letter, and there are probably lots of them. I did start a search, but I don't remember if I checked to see if the results have come up. I've been a little busy."

"I get that," she's said, "but I think it's important."

"I might be able to tap in from here. I'll call you back." He disappeared on the phone as soon as he said that.

Doreen made herself a cup of tea and stared out moodily. This case was about to crack wide open, and she had a pretty damn good idea what was going on, but she just didn't know how. She settled down again and looked up Lynette's address. That was the one person who needed a good talking to. She was the one hiding secrets. Or maybe she didn't give a damn. She certainly hadn't waited before she remarried. So, who knew what was going on there?

Doreen found the address, looked it up, and realized it was a ten-minute drive away. As she sat here, doing nothing anyway, she thought, *What the heck?* She stood and grabbed her keys.

Then Mugs raced past her, and Thaddeus cried behind her, "Thaddeus come. Thaddeus come." Even Goliath sauntered in to see what was happening.

She stopped with a groan and said, "Really? Do we all have to go?"

Chapter 32

Wednesday Late Afternoon ...

MUGS BARKED SEVERAL times, and Doreen laughed. "Okay," she said. "Fine. It's a road trip."

With all three animals in her car again, Doreen backed down the driveway and out of the cul-de-sac, heading toward Gordon Avenue. Finally she turned toward Dilworth Road and used it to cut across the mall area to Dilworth Mountain. In her mind, she understood where she was supposed to go, but some of the streets didn't sound familiar. She took several corners and then finally came to the right street. And shortly afterward, she came to the house in question. It was a huge all-brick mansion and looked timeless. It sat there, just off to the corner, where it would maximize the view of the city below.

Doreen nodded to herself, pulled up and around, parked, got out with the animals, and decided she'd take a casual walk past. She was walking on the other side when a Mercedes pulled into the driveway. Their big garage door opened, and the Mercedes pulled in beside a truck. This made Doreen stop in her tracks.

"It pulled up beside a black truck," she whispered to herself. She hurriedly pulled out her phone and called Mack.

"I haven't had a chance to get an answer yet," he snapped at her.

"New search," she said, her voice steadily soft. "Look up Norbert's wife's new husband's vehicles. She just parked her Mercedes in her garage beside a black truck."

Mack swore on the other end of the phone.

She cut him off, saying, "Yes, I'm here. Yes, I'm looking. Yes, I have a damn good idea what happened, and you need to get me some proof."

Then she hung up on him and walked around the cul-de-sac a couple times before putting the animals back into her vehicle and sitting with them, wondering what she should do now. She needed the woman's number. Using her cell phone, she tried to track it down but didn't get anywhere. It was probably unlisted. She needed Mack to get that too. And that would just piss him off.

Finally she decided to leave her car, taking Mugs and Goliath on their leashes and Thaddeus on her shoulder. She walked up to the front door and rang the doorbell. It was one of those elegant executive homes her ex would have loved. She'd lived in plenty of them herself too, but they didn't appeal to her. They always had that modern contemporary look but were very cold feeling. When the door opened, a beautifully coiffed blonde stood in front of her with a bored look on her face.

The woman reminded Doreen of her past. All the women she'd known back then had the same elegance and the same bored look.

She asked, "Yes?"

Doreen gave her a bright smile and with a blunt tone said, "I just wondered why you tried to pay Manny money to leave town."

The woman stared at her, and fear whispered through her eyes.

Doreen nodded and added, "Exactly. Did you think it would all just go away?"

The woman looked around hurriedly. "You better come in," she said, as she pulled the door open.

Doreen stepped inside with the animals in tow. A beautiful slate floor with some high-gloss finish made the entire room glow. But Doreen had seen much nicer. She was completely unimpressed if the woman was trying to intimidate her. Doreen had the wrong person in that regard. "So you haven't answered my question."

"Why the hell should I?" the woman snapped, showing the ugliness that lived inside. "It's got nothing to do with you."

"I get that you might not like that your first husband was banging Manny on a regular basis. Weekly, to be exact, but what difference did it make at that point if Manny was still around or not?"

The woman stared at her in horror. "How could you possibly know all this?"

"I also know," Doreen said, "that Norbert was being charged with stealing from the bank."

"No, no, no." The woman shook her head. "He wasn't charged. That's the thing. They were going to lay him off, but they weren't going to charge him."

"So, what? You couldn't handle it? You couldn't handle the humiliation?"

"What are you talking about?"

"You couldn't handle it, so you ran him down?"

"I didn't run him down," she said. "How dare you accuse me!"

"Why not? Manny disappears. Norbert dies in a hit-and-run, and a month later here you are, married and up another step on the social ladder." Doreen waved her arm around at the house for emphasis.

The woman's face turned blotchy red with anger, and she stomped her foot on the floor. "You don't know anything about it," she said. "Do you have any idea what it's like when your husband wants to spend time with a prostitute? Like, how absolutely disgusting is that?"

"I think Manny was probably a very nice person," Doreen said.

"How could she/he be," Lynette snapped. "*It* was an abomination."

"Right," Doreen said, hating how this woman had reduced Manny to an *it*. "So you killed *him*."

The woman laughed. And the thing was, it was real laughter.

Doreen's heart sank, as she realized she'd been wrong.

"I didn't have anything to do with *her*. I tried to give her money, hoping she'd leave town and save me the humiliation that all my friends knew about. It was bad enough Norbert was being let go from the bank with a cloud of suspicion over him," she said tiredly—her shiny good looks slipping into a brassiness, showing the tarnish over her years. "But to think he was doing whatever he was doing with *that* person, God!" She shook her head in disbelief.

"And your marriage a month after Norbert died?" Doreen asked.

"Oh, you should know," the woman said snidely. "I understand your husband dumped you. So you went from having it all to having nothing. Well, I was done with having nothing—I wanted at all."

Doreen's heart sank farther as she realized this woman already knew a lot of Doreen's history and probably half the town did too. Doreen said, "You were married so fast. You were probably banging him while your husband was banging poor Manny."

"*Poor Manny*," she snapped. "They'd known each other for forever. He kept trying to defend his lifestyle and saying he was just mixed up and needed support." She shook her head. "It's disgusting."

Doreen wasn't of the same mind-set. "And your second husband, did he mind all that?"

"Of course," she said, "He wanted it all to go away himself."

"Of course he did," Doreen said with a thin smile, not believing half of what Lynette said. "I guess, since Norbert died, life's been good, right?"

"Why shouldn't it be?" the woman snapped. "I mean, I went through hell before my husband died. It was a relief when he was gone. And Manny too. You have no idea what it's like to be the object of ridicule."

"Actually I do," Doreen said. "Not for the same reasons, but I definitely understand being laughed at."

"Then why are you even asking me all this? It's so long ago."

"Because they found Manny's body," Doreen said.

The woman looked at her in horror.

"That's right. They found his body. And forensics is all over it."

The woman stepped back, her hand going to her chest. "You don't think I had something to do with it, do you?"

Doreen raised an eyebrow. She'd learned long ago that

people often shot off their mouths if you gave them a chance to talk.

The woman shook her head. "Why would I bother? Manny had been in my husband's life for so long it was a humiliating nightmare. But it was just one more disgusting part of the life I had to live."

"You could have left," Doreen said.

"I considered it," Lynette said. "You bet I did. And then Dean came along."

Lynette told Doreen the last part with a smile, a smile that said she got sucked in and fell in love. It told Doreen that Dean had taken Lynette away, like the charming prince he appeared to be, and had converted her life from hell to heaven.

Doreen nodded. "I guess he didn't think much of any of it, did he?"

"No, he told me that I should leave Norbert. That I should leave it all behind."

"So why didn't you?"

"I didn't know how," Lynette said simply. "It would just be so messy."

"Getting up one day, walking out of the house, and moving in with your new boyfriend, is it *that* messy?"

"You don't understand," the woman said briskly, "but I had nothing to do with Manny's death."

Just then a voice behind them called out, "Sweetheart, is everything okay?"

Chapter 33

Wednesday Dinnertime ...

LYNETTE BEAMED AND ran past Doreen, who spun to look at the tall silver-haired gentleman in the doorway. He caught Lynette and kissed her gently, then looked at Doreen, and asked, "Are you harassing my wife?"

"Not at all," Doreen said with a bright smile. "Just asking her questions about her role in Manny's death."

The man's face turned sheer white. "What? What did you just say?"

"But she clarified a few points for me," Doreen said. "She said she wasn't involved, and I believe her now. It was done by your hands alone."

The man protested. Lynette turned to Doreen and said, "What?"

Doreen nodded. "You wouldn't leave your husband. Your husband was a disgrace. Manny was something that shouldn't even be allowed to exist according to you, so Dean took them both out of the equation with that lovely black truck," she said. "The black truck you no longer drive, right? The one without a license plate that's in the garage?"

He shook his head slowly, like a bull in a china shop,

preparing to charge. Doreen held up her hand and said, "Stop. Don't even bother. The cops found Manny's body. They're all over the forensics on it now."

If she'd thought Dean'd been white before, now he had almost translucent skin.

She turned to Lynette and motioned to Dean's face. "See? *Guilt.* He gets Manny to come with him by pretending to be a john, takes him out, kills him, and buries him out at Paul's Tomb. After that, he waits a few days and hits Norbert with his truck. Norbert doesn't survive, and everything's all free and clear. Hell, Norbert probably was stealing from the bank to finance his escape with Manny. Did you grab the money from his car at the same time? You get to keep your assets, and, within thirty days, he's got you locked up tight as his wife. Nobody's the wiser." She turned to face Dean. "What do you call it? *Taking out the trash?*"

"That's not bad," Dean said. His voice was a deep growl, as if some rage was building inside. "That's a pretty story. Not that it matters. Neither one of them deserved to live."

"I'm sure your wife agreed with you."

Lynette stared at her husband, then back at Doreen. Then she took a step back. "Is that right, Dean? Did you run poor Norbert down?"

"*Poor Norbert?* That man wasn't a man, he was a two-timing thief," he snapped. "You know perfectly well you wanted him dead."

"He was under suspicion for stealing from the bank. He was having sex with that thing on the streets and bringing home every disease possible. Of course I was unhappy. But I didn't want him killed."

"So you would have been happy if he had just died from a heart attack or some major disease?" Doreen asked.

The woman nodded. "Exactly. I wanted it all to go away but didn't want him killed."

"Too bad," Doreen said cheerfully. "Because Dean did it for you."

The woman stared at Doreen and back at Dean. She shook her head. "Please tell me that you didn't. *Please. Please, tell me.*" She reached up to gently cup his cheeks. "I've loved you for so long. Please tell me that you didn't do this."

"Everything I've done, I did for you," he said brokenly to Lynette. "Because you wouldn't leave him, I *had* to."

Through the open front door, Doreen could see several vehicles pulling up, sirens blazing.

Dean didn't even bother glancing behind him.

Doreen smiled. "Well, you'll get to say it all over again many times," she said, "because here's your ride."

Dean glared at her and said, "Do you think I'll just walk out of here?" He stiffened his back, straightened up, and said, "It's your word against mine. The cops can go over the truck. I don't care."

"Not just my word against you," she said. "We have a lot of witnesses now. And, of course, Manny is just now telling his story too."

Dean grimaced at the thought and shook his head. "You don't know anything."

"I know that Manny struggled," she said. "Manny fought for his life. And, at the very end, you wouldn't even give him the mercy of being found so his family could mourn. And then, when you came back from killing Manny, you were completely casual about the whole thing and never said a word to anybody. After that, you plotted poor Norbert's downfall. And that was way too easy, wasn't it?

"Now here, ten years later, you've got it all. You've got the fancy house, the beautiful wife, the great job—you're the king of your castle." Doreen gave them a smile that would put anybody on edge. Except for Dean, because he was too arrogant to see it. "But you built it all on a crumbling foundation. You made it out of murder and lies."

Lynette gripped his hands and whispered, "Please tell me the truth."

He reached down gently, kissed her on the forehead, and said, "Don't worry about it."

"You noticed he never said *no*," Doreen said cheerfully.

Lynette looked at Doreen, then at her husband. "Dean, I want you to tell me right now by looking in my eyes."

He smiled and cupped her cheek. "Why would you even listen to this woman?"

"See?" Doreen said. "Once again, he didn't say no."

Behind him, she could see Mack walking up the sidewalk. Several other men headed to the garage. She looked at Dean and said, "You can't say it because it's a lie, and you can't lie to her because you love her. You killed her husband just to free her up so she could be with you."

Dean stared at his wife, and his shoulders sagged. He slowly whispered, "I killed him. I had to. You wouldn't leave him. You wouldn't leave that lousy sniveling little worm for me. I had to do something."

Lynette shook her head, her hand clasped over her mouth, as she cried, "No, no, please, no."

He reached out for her, but she took a step back.

Doreen was just about to congratulate herself on having gotten one case closed without actually getting hurt, when Dean turned, grabbed something from the sideboard that held his keys, and swung it in Doreen's direction. She took a glass bowl hard in her chest, crying out as she stumbled back, falling to the floor. Thaddeus squawked and flew free. She was okay, but it knocked the wind out of her.

She could hear Lynette screaming in the background and asking Dean to stop. But he picked up something else and lunged toward Doreen to smash it into her. As he took two steps, Mugs jumped at him. Only Dean kicked Mugs away. Mugs fell over, whining, as Goliath lunged upward, digging his claws into Dean's lean belly. Dean roared and tried to brush Goliath off, but Mugs was back at Dean again.

Not to be outdone, Thaddeus flew onto Dean's distinguished hair, sending it flying everywhere. He dug his claws in and pecked away. Dean roared in anger, frustration, and pain, as the animals attacked him at all once.

And finally, over all of it, Doreen felt warm arms wrap around her and help her to her feet.

Mack's voice came through the din. "Are you okay?"

She looked up at him gratefully and nodded. "I will be."

"Good. You might want to call off your defenders then, please."

She gave a sharp whistle, and Mugs returned to her side, while Goliath shot her a look, as if to say, *It was really getting good now.* But still, he dropped from Dean's midsection to the floor and sauntered toward her. Then Mack scooped up Thaddeus and plunked him on Doreen's shoulder, while they all watched the wreckage of the man in front of them, crying. Dean was still standing, but he was torn and bleeding.

"Looks like Doreen strikes again," Mack said.

Two cops behind him chuckled. "Looks like Doreen and her *army* strike again," they said.

Doreen looked over at Mack and said, "The black

truck's in the garage. You know that, right?"

"I know it now," he said.

"I don't think Lynette had anything to do with any of the killings, but she tipped me off."

Lynette stared at Doreen. "What are you talking about?"

"You paid Manny money to disappear," Doreen said. "That made no sense."

"How could it not make sense? She was humiliating me! My life was a mess because of her. How could it not make sense to get rid of her?"

"Sure, but somebody *did* get rid of him," Doreen corrected. "And, if it wasn't you, then who? It had to be somebody who cared. And that led me to the man who loved you enough to kill for you. But, once he got rid of one nasty irritant in *your* life, he got rid of the one nasty irritant in *his* life." She glanced at the animals huddled close to her side. "You see? When you love someone, you'd do almost anything to save them."

"But not murder," Mack said, with a note of warning.

Doreen laughed. "Never murder. Besides, whoever threw all that stuff into Richard's garden, they had no idea what they started. Handcuffs in the heather, indeed."

"Yeah, so now what? Something starting with *I*?"

"I hope not," she said with a shudder. "The only thing that comes to mind is *ice*. Don't like the sound of that. I'm a sun-loving girl. Don't like the cold much."

"Then don't think about it," Mack said comfortably. "Maybe you're done now. Got all this amateur sleuth stuff out of your system."

"If that's the only other option," she said, as she scowled at him, "I'll take ice. After all, how hard could it be? The big lake freezes over here, so maybe someone else is lost in the lake."

Mack rolled his eyes at her. "Knowing you, you'll compound the issue and make it an ice pick as the murder weapon."

She glared at him. "Knowing me …? Is that an insult?"

He laughed. "Come on. Let's get you home. Whatever the next case is, it's not today's issue."

Doreen let him lead her out to her car, and, instead of helping her in, he took her around to the passenger side and loaded her and the animals up, then got in on the driver's side. She had to admit, she was a little shaky. So being driven home was a novelty she would enjoy. Besides it gave her time to consider ice picks. Not a bad idea at all …

Epilogue

Friday Noon …

T HREE DAYS. ALL Doreen had wanted was three days of peace and quiet. At least that's what she thought she wanted. But by noon on day two, she was bored out of her mind. She sat on her small deck with a cup of coffee in her hand, but her foot kept tapping the floorboards.

Finally she jumped up. "This is ridiculous," she announced to Mugs, who was sprawled out in the sunshine beside her. "We have to get some work done. It's either that or I'll go stir-crazy." She bounded off the deck steps, wondering where her now-full energy level had come from. Yesterday she'd been dragging her sorry butt around the kitchen and trying hard to put all the pieces in her head into place. But now, well, now she was full of energy and ready to go.

She grabbed the shovel and headed to the garden to start on the next bed. She kept looking back at the markers that were still in her lawn to show where the expanded deck was supposed to go. She hadn't done anything further because, of course, it would be not just her working; it would also require Mack. Was a project this size doable on a weekend or

DALE MAYER

several weekends?

Today was Friday, and normally she would be gardening at Millicent's, but Millicent had again asked Doreen to come on a Saturday instead. After weeks of working on Mack's mother's yard, Millicent's garden was looking decent. So, unless Millicent or Mack had anything extra they needed Doreen to do, it would probably just be two hours, tops, of weeding to keep the gardens in perfect shape.

And Doreen didn't really want to drop her income, but she also didn't feel good about taking money for three hours if she was only putting in two.

With her first kick onto the shovel, digging into her own backyard, she could feel that same satisfaction rolling through her. She loved working her own land. She loved working on this place. As she moved closer to the house, she looked down at Mugs to see he had not moved. "You're just being lazy."

Mugs opened his eyes but didn't budge. She looked to see Goliath sprawled on the grass behind her, his tail twitching.

"Well, at least you're here beside me," she said. She bent down, lifted a clump of weeds, gave it a good shake, tossed it off to one side to create a new pile, and kept working as she headed down the right side of her property. Then she realized she had seen no recent sign of Thaddeus.

She turned and looked around. "Thaddeus? Thaddeus, where are you?"

There was a flutter of wings, and Thaddeus muttered, "Thaddeus is here. Thaddeus is here."

She spun around to see him waddling toward her from the creek. "You know you're not supposed to go to the creek on your own," she scolded him. "Not with it rising like it has been."

He just squawked and gave a full-winged feather ruffle. She laughed. "Like you care what I say."

Looking closely then, she caught a glint of something in front of him on the ground.

"What did you find?" She stabbed her shovel into the dirt and headed toward him. But, instead of being cooperative, he picked up the small object and bounced backward.

"No, no, Thaddeus, we're not making a game out of this."

But Thaddeus wasn't listening—he was too enthralled with whatever it was he'd found.

She glared at him, knowing the more she chased him, the more he would back up or fly away.

Goliath walked to her side, studying Thaddeus with great interest.

"You're not allowed to go after him," Doreen snapped at Goliath. He just gave her a slow-eyed look, as if to say, *Seriously?*

At that, Thaddeus stopped and stared at both of them.

"Thaddeus, come here," Doreen said, and she crouched in front of him.

Thaddeus started to back away, and Goliath crouched down low, as if to pounce. She put a hand on top of Goliath's back and neck and said, "We don't do that to friends."

He made a weird chittering sound, and she tapped him gently on the nose. "Goliath, behave yourself."

Thaddeus hopped forward, as if willing to give her whatever was in his beak. It was metal and small. She didn't understand, but it looked like a label.

"That's cool, Thaddeus," she said, as she held out a hand.

He looked at her, cocked his head to the side, and then dropped it.

Doreen snatched it up before he could change his mind. She looked at it, noting the little indents. It was like a little nameplate or something for a tool. "I don't have a clue what it means but thank you."

She popped it into her pocket, got back up, and returned to her digging.

Only Thaddeus wasn't happy with that. He squawked at her, "Thaddeus. Thaddeus."

"What's the matter, Thaddeus?"

He hopped away a few steps. She frowned, dug the shovel deep into the ground again, and took another few steps toward him. Immediately he hopped back toward the creek. "Oh, that's not good," she said. "Please tell me that you didn't find any more bodies."

He just turned, gave her that gimlet eye, and kept going.

She walked around to the end of the path, where the creek flowed but the water level was much lower. She stared at the creek water, absolutely loving the trickling sounds. She asked, "So what were you looking at?"

Thaddeus hopped over, but he still looked like he wanted her to follow. With her heart sinking, she walked toward the little bridge as Thaddeus hopped across the wooden slats. "Thaddeus, careful, we never fixed that side."

He called back, "Thaddeus is fine. Thaddeus is fine."

She laughed, and, with Goliath's and finally Mugs's attention, she carefully made her way across the bridge. "We'll have to get Mack to give us a hand with this," she said. "I know it's city property, but surely they wouldn't mind if we fixed the broken boards." As she was the one who had gone through the wood, she would at least like to stop herself from falling through a second time. On the other side of the creek Thaddeus headed toward the lake.

"Thaddeus, that's not good," she said. "I don't want to take a walk now."

But he only went a little farther, and then he stopped.

She came up behind him and saw a second glint. And there was another little nameplate. She frowned, bent down, picked it up, and studied it. She then pulled the first one from her pocket and said, "Weird. They are the same." One was slightly bigger though.

Thaddeus hopped onto her foot. She reached down, placed her palms so he could hop on them, and then lifted the bird to let him glide up to her shoulder. Once he was settled there, he crooned gently and rubbed his beak against her cheek. "Thank you for these shiny gifts," she murmured, chuckling as she gently stroked his feathers.

She studied the nameplates curiously. "What are these, and what the devil do they have to do with us?"

Of course she knew. Likely they had something to do with a new case—whether she was ready or not.

This concludes Book 8 of Lovely Lethal Gardens:
Handcuffs in the Heather.
Read about Ice Pick in the Ivy:
Lovely Lethal Gardens, Book 9

Lovely Lethal Gardens: Ice Pick in the Ivy (Book #9)

A new cozy mystery series from *USA Today* best-selling author Dale Mayer. Follow gardener and amateur sleuth Doreen Montgomery—and her amusing and mostly lovable cat, dog, and parrot—as they catch murderers and solve crimes in lovely Kelowna, British Columbia.

Riches to rags. … Chaos never calms. … Time fades memories. … Or at least most of them!

Who knew two small maker's marks could lead to such chaos? Doreen has been enjoying a few well-earned days of peace and quiet after solving her last mystery. But all good things must come to an end. Like when Thaddeus, her independently minded African gray parrot, digs up two rectangular metal pieces from the path along the creek. Then Doreen is sent down another rabbit hole of the past: connecting the dots from a long-defunct tool repair company and a young girl who disappeared at the same time.

Corporal Mack Moreau doesn't think these events are connected. He doesn't believe the spate of recent deaths is suspiciously tied in either. Mack wants Doreen to focus on the materials and the cost analysis to replace her backyard deck and to leave the detecting to him. But how can she, when she knows so much more is going on than Mack believes?

Heart attacks, unfair wills, and a missing ice pick are all related. She just needs to understand how …

Find Book 9 here!
To find out more visit Dale Mayer's website.
https://geni.us/DMIcepickUniversal

Author's Note

Thank you for reading Handcuffs in the Heather: Lovely Lethal Gardens, Book 8! If you enjoyed the book, please take a moment and leave a short review.

Dear reader,

I love to hear from readers, and you can contact me at my website: www.dalemayer.com or at my Facebook author page. To be informed of new releases and special offers, sign up for my newsletter or follow me on BookBub. And if you are interested in joining Dale Mayer's Reader Group, here is the Facebook sign up page.
http://geni.us/DaleMayerFBGroup

Cheers,
Dale Mayer

About the Author

Dale Mayer is a *USA Today* best-selling author, best known for her SEALs military romances, her Psychic Visions series, and her Lovely Lethal Garden cozy series. Her contemporary romances are raw and full of passion and emotion (Broken But … Mending, Hathaway House series). Her thrillers will keep you guessing (Kate Morgan, By Death series), and her romantic comedies will keep you giggling (*It's a Dog's Life*, a stand-alone novella; and the Broken Protocols series, starring Charming Marvin, the cat).

Dale honors the stories that come to her—and some of them are crazy, break all the rules and cross multiple genres!

To go with her fiction, she also writes nonfiction in many different fields, with books available on résumé writing, companion gardening, and the US mortgage system. All her books are available in print and ebook format.

Connect with Dale Mayer Online

Dale's Website – www.dalemayer.com
Twitter – @DaleMayer
Facebook Page – geni.us/DaleMayerFBFanPage
Facebook Group – geni.us/DaleMayerFBGroup
BookBub – geni.us/DaleMayerBookbub
Instagram – geni.us/DaleMayerInstagram
Goodreads – geni.us/DaleMayerGoodreads
Newsletter – geni.us/DaleNews

Also by Dale Mayer

Published Adult Books:

Hathaway House
Aaron, Book 1
Brock, Book 2
Cole, Book 3
Denton, Book 4
Elliot, Book 5
Finn, Book 6
Gregory, Book 7
Heath, Book 8
Iain, Book 9

The K9 Files
Ethan, Book 1
Pierce, Book 2
Zane, Book 3
Blaze, Book 4
Lucas, Book 5
Parker, Book 6
Carter, Book 7

Lovely Lethal Gardens
Arsenic in the Azaleas, Book 1
Bones in the Begonias, Book 2
Corpse in the Carnations, Book 3

Daggers in the Dahlias, Book 4
Evidence in the Echinacea, Book 5
Footprints in the Ferns, Book 6
Gun in the Gardenias, Book 7
Handcuffs in the Heather, Book 8
Ice Pick in the Ivy, Book 9

Psychic Vision Series
Tuesday's Child
Hide 'n Go Seek
Maddy's Floor
Garden of Sorrow
Knock Knock...
Rare Find
Eyes to the Soul
Now You See Her
Shattered
Into the Abyss
Seeds of Malice
Eye of the Falcon
Itsy-Bitsy Spider
Unmasked
Deep Beneath
From the Ashes
Stroke of Death
Psychic Visions Books 1–3
Psychic Visions Books 4–6
Psychic Visions Books 7–9

By Death Series
Touched by Death
Haunted by Death

Chilled by Death
By Death Books 1–3

Broken Protocols – Romantic Comedy Series
Cat's Meow
Cat's Pajamas
Cat's Cradle
Cat's Claus
Broken Protocols 1-4

Broken and... Mending
Skin
Scars
Scales (of Justice)
Broken but... Mending 1-3

Glory
Genesis
Tori
Celeste
Glory Trilogy

Biker Blues
Morgan: Biker Blues, Volume 1
Cash: Biker Blues, Volume 2

SEALs of Honor
Mason: SEALs of Honor, Book 1
Hawk: SEALs of Honor, Book 2
Dane: SEALs of Honor, Book 3
Swede: SEALs of Honor, Book 4
Shadow: SEALs of Honor, Book 5
Cooper: SEALs of Honor, Book 6

Markus: SEALs of Honor, Book 7
Evan: SEALs of Honor, Book 8
Mason's Wish: SEALs of Honor, Book 9
Chase: SEALs of Honor, Book 10
Brett: SEALs of Honor, Book 11
Devlin: SEALs of Honor, Book 12
Easton: SEALs of Honor, Book 13
Ryder: SEALs of Honor, Book 14
Macklin: SEALs of Honor, Book 15
Corey: SEALs of Honor, Book 16
Warrick: SEALs of Honor, Book 17
Tanner: SEALs of Honor, Book 18
Jackson: SEALs of Honor, Book 19
Kanen: SEALs of Honor, Book 20
Nelson: SEALs of Honor, Book 21
Taylor: SEALs of Honor, Book 22
Colton: SEALs of Honor, Book 23
SEALs of Honor, Books 1–3
SEALs of Honor, Books 4–6
SEALs of Honor, Books 7–10
SEALs of Honor, Books 11–13
SEALs of Honor, Books 14–16
SEALs of Honor, Books 17–19

Heroes for Hire

Levi's Legend: Heroes for Hire, Book 1
Stone's Surrender: Heroes for Hire, Book 2
Merk's Mistake: Heroes for Hire, Book 3
Rhodes's Reward: Heroes for Hire, Book 4
Flynn's Firecracker: Heroes for Hire, Book 5
Logan's Light: Heroes for Hire, Book 6
Harrison's Heart: Heroes for Hire, Book 7

SEALs of Steel

SEALs of Steel, Books 1–8

The Mavericks
Kerrick, Book 1
Griffin, Book 2
Jax, Book 3
Beau, Book 4
Asher, Book 5
Ryker, Book 6
Miles, Book 7
Nico, Book 8
Keane, Book 9
Lennox, Book 10
Gavin, Book 11
Shane, Book 12

Bullard's Battle Series
Ryland's Reach, Book 1
Cain's Cross, Book 2
Eton's Escape, Book 3
Garret's Gambit, Book 4
Kano's Keep, Book 5
Fallon's Flaw, Book 6
Quinn's Quest, Book 7
Bullard's Beauty, Book 8

Collections
Dare to Be You…
Dare to Love…
Dare to be Strong…
RomanceX3

Standalone Novellas
It's a Dog's Life
Riana's Revenge
Second Chances

Published Young Adult Books:

Family Blood Ties Series
Vampire in Denial
Vampire in Distress
Vampire in Design
Vampire in Deceit
Vampire in Defiance
Vampire in Conflict
Vampire in Chaos
Vampire in Crisis
Vampire in Control
Vampire in Charge
Family Blood Ties Set 1–3
Family Blood Ties Set 1–5
Family Blood Ties Set 4–6
Family Blood Ties Set 7–9
Sian's Solution, A Family Blood Ties Series Prequel
    Novelette

Design series
Dangerous Designs
Deadly Designs
Darkest Designs
Design Series Trilogy

Standalone

In Cassie's Corner
Gem Stone (a Gemma Stone Mystery)
Time Thieves

Published Non-Fiction Books:

Career Essentials

Career Essentials: The Résumé
Career Essentials: The Cover Letter
Career Essentials: The Interview
Career Essentials: 3 in 1